A DIZZYING D...

Not even the most whirling waltz had left Corinna's head spinning so dizzyingly as the position in which she now found herself.

Leaning over her, taking her hand in his, was the most powerful man in Europe, the czar of Russia, Emperor Alexander himself. The jewels he had sent her, and the gleam now in his eyes, made no secret of what he wanted.

Coming toward her, the expression on his handsome face making clear his intention to rescue her, was Justin Farrington, Lord Lonsdale.

This was her chance, then, to make sure that Lonsdale would never again come near enough to make her senses reel and trouble her conscience.

All she had to do to drive away this man she was honor-bound to reject was to risk her virtue with a ruler who knew no law but his own desire....

The Errant Bridegroom

Vanessa Gray
The Errant Bridegroom

A SIGNET BOOK

NEW AMERICAN LIBRARY

NAL BOOKS ARE AVAILABLE AT QUANTITY DISCOUNTS
WHEN USED TO PROMOTE PRODUCTS OR SERVICES.
FOR INFORMATION PLEASE WRITE TO PREMIUM MARKETING DIVISION,
NEW AMERICAN LIBRARY, 1633 BROADWAY,
NEW YORK, NEW YORK 10019.

SIGNET, SIGNET CLASSIC, MENTOR, PLUME, MERIDIAN
and NAL BOOKS are published by New American Library,
1633 Broadway, New York, New York 10019

First Printing, March, 1986

1   2   3   4   5   6   7   8   9

PRINTED IN THE UNITED STATES OF AMERICA

CHAPTER 1

The November sun broke through heavy overhanging clouds and shone weakly down on the little wooded hills of Kent, giving small warmth and less encouragement to the landscape.

Winter was on the way, without question—and only the optimistic pointed out that at least the interminable wars on the Continent were over and all that remained to do was to dispose of the debris left by Napoleon's heavy-footed armies and heavier-handed politics. That chore was at this moment being taken care of in Vienna by the victors, since Bonaparte himself was safely imprisoned in his shabby palace on Elba—and reported to be happy in his exile, although certain of the more astute among the victorious diplomats remembered the emperor's promise: "I will be with you when the spring flowers bloom again."

But now it was only November, and the flowers of spring were sleeping. Even the sunshine seemed to hold a feeling of lassitude, as though its spring chores were too far in the future to contemplate. Frail as it was, the sunshine could not penetrate the heavy woodlands encroaching on the parkland of Morland Hall, situated at the head of a pleasant, sheltered valley.

Truly, shade was kinder to Morland Hall than was bright light. In the shadows, the structure returned briefly to its old grandeur. A three-story building of stone, with an imposing pillared entrance, it looked with shuttered eyes down the valley.

Only at close hand could a critical visitor notice lichen growing on the stones of the walls, flecks of paint like new snow at the base of the pillars, and saplings straying unmolested into the park. The last occasion on which the graveled drive had been raked was beyond memory.

However, the signs of neglect on the outside of Morland Hall were, at least at this moment, of little interest to the two ladies lingering in the morning room over breakfast.

Miss Corinna Darley was the younger of the two, having reached the near-spinster age of twenty-three. She was dressed in a modest round gown of blue kerseymere, not in the latest mode. Indeed, one might think she was not aware of the newest fashions from London either in dress or in hairdressing. One would be nearer the mark to judge that although she possessed a dress allowance sufficiently large to indulge herself in fashion, she considered that her retired country life, especially during this year of mourning for her stepfather, called for nothing more than neatness and decency. The more elegant forms of dress were, as she told Emma, simply a nuisance in walking out over the grounds or climbing fences, and how did one ever manage to hold on to one's bonnet in a high wind, to say nothing of inserting one's head into a carriage?

Corinna had no illusions as to her beauty, but she was far from plain. Her hair was the dark blond color of a dried beech leaf. Her great charm, however, lay in her thin, intelligent face and her speaking hazel eyes, which looked at the world with an amused and lively expression.

At the moment, in truth, sufficient funds were

on her mind. She buttered the last bit of toast and frowned at it as though it had in some way disappointed her. Setting it down on her plate, she turned to her companion.

"Emma, my dear," she said to Miss Sanford, erstwhile governess, now chaperon to Corinna's stepsister, Almira Morland, and companion to Corinna herself, "I think we must talk. I have done the most reprehensible thing! I do hope you will not scold me overmuch."

"I cannot imagine that I should, my dear," said Emma placidly. "I do not recall that I was charged with overseeing your deportment."

Corinna smiled. "Of course not. But you know I do value your opinion."

"Until it comes to young Miss Almira herself," Emma pointed out. "I confess there are times when I should wish to shut her up in the attic. Do you think bread and water would have a salutary effect on that young miss?"

"I doubt she listens to anyone but Jack Hardie. I cannot abandon her, you know." Corinna's argument was not set forth for the first time. "I remember Sir Rupert's kindness to me too well."

"I am not urging you," said Emma, "to be ungrateful. It is only that Almira is letting her new freedom carry her to outrageous lengths."

"I collect you have Jack Hardie on your mind. He is only a playfellow." She saw Emma's lips tighten disapprovingly. "Very well, not a playfellow. But he is younger than I am."

"By only one year. However, he is six years older than Almira, and I cannot condone such ramshackle behavior as haring off across the country day after day."

Corinna protested. "He cannot have it in mind to

seduce her! She is a wellborn young lady, and he would not dare!"

"I should be loath to suspect him of giving her a slip on the shoulder—"

"Where did you learn such language?"

Ignoring her, Emma continued, "—but I confess I do not quite like her headlong infatuation with him."

"There is no one else for her to ride out with."

"I have a bit more experience than you, dear Corinna, and I suspect all young men of placing undue value on the satisfaction of their own wishes."

"But not to the detriment of a young lady of quality! Would he not fear retribution?"

Emma said, with simple practicality, "From whom? Mr. Treffingham?"

The absurd notion of their London trustee, the thin, tottery, dry-as-dust Mr. Ebenezer Treffingham, challenging the brutish Jack Hardie to a duel reduced Corinna to giggles.

"Just the same," she said at last, "I cannot think that Jack would hazard his future for an hour of—of dalliance!"

"I cannot agree, my dear. If she did accede to his wishes, what would happen? He would be forced to marry her, I suppose. And perhaps that is his goal?"

"Do you really think—?"

"One has only to look at his father," Emma pointed out.

She had touched upon the one cogent factor that gave Corinna reason to believe the arguments Emma had advanced over the past few weeks. Sir Edward Hardie was a notorious rake, who was subsiding now into an alcoholic nonentity with lively memories of past conquests and former wildnesses.

"What shall we ever do?"

Emma Sanford was a woman of uncertain years

and comfortable appearance. Long ago perceiving that her days were likely to be spent in the half-world—neither servant nor lady—of a governess, she had reasonably decided that she would accept what indulgences came her way, without questioning them. Second only to her intense love of music, her pleasure was taken at the table, as her ample figure bore witness.

She was nonetheless an educated woman of excellent breeding, if lacking in family and resources, and—to Corinna's constant pleasure—possessed of a bottomless store of good nature, seasoned with a kind of wry humor.

For the rest, she had a wealth of fine light brown hair forever escaping from its anchoring pins, and eyes of such a light blue as to be nearly colorless. A face so bland as to be unmemorable, thought Corinna, until one noticed the great kindness in her expression.

"Eat your toast first, I would say," Emma said calmly, "and finish up the pot of coffee. How you can endure that bitter taste of mocha in the morning, I do not know."

Corinna placed her hand on the side of the pot and frowned. "I'll ask Brixton to bring a fresh pot in a moment. Just now I want to talk to you."

"Ah, yes, you were going to tell me of the reprehensible thing you have done?"

Corinna did not answer directly. Seemingly at a tangent, she said, "It has been nearly a year since Sir Rupert died, and something must be done."

"About what?"

"About Almira."

Emma smiled wryly. "She is all we talk about, it seems. The only thing you can do for her is to leave her and set up your own household."

"I cannot."

"I know that. But I hope you are about to tell me that you have written to Lady Hardie protesting her son's attentions to your stepsister."

"Do you think that would do any good at all?" said Corinna. "No, Emma. I have done something much worse."

"You have insulted the vicar's wife," suggested Emma. "No? Then I have it—you have told Lady Hardie that Treffie has absconded with Almira's dowry. Shall we expect a shocked visit from Lady Hardie?" She glanced out of the window as though she expected the Hardie carriage to be already coming into view.

"I certainly hope not," exclaimed Corinna. "I confess that woman wearies me beyond endurance. Telling me what I am not so hen-witted as not to know—"

"Pray tell me that again!"

"You know what I mean!" Corinna laughed. "I *know* what should be done with Almira, and I do not need the advice of a lady whose only claim to expertness in rearing children is that great oaf Jack!"

The two fell silent, contemplating the young man who loomed so large in their thoughts. Jack Hardie was the only son of Sir Edward and Lady Hardie, and an awkward young man of few manners. He was of short stature, and made up for this defect by lording it over the nearby villagers. Although he was all of six years older than Almira, he had always shown a protective attitude toward her, the only other young person of his class in the neighborhood, and Corinna believed her stepsister safe with him.

"She is sixteen now," resumed Corinna, as though talking to herself. "My mother always deemed it uwise to bring a young lady out until she was of an age not to be addled by undue masculine pressures.

I know, though, that it is considered quite acceptable to come out when one reaches the age of seventeen, and in Almira's case, I think the sooner the better. She deserves a Season, and she must find a husband. But how can that be accomplished when we are forty miles from town, and there is not a female of our acquaintance who would be able to sponsor her?"

"Has she complained?"

"No," confessed Corinna, frowning, "she hasn't. But it has never occurred her to take the slightest thought for the future—even for the next sennight. You know I have no authority to arrange for her coming out, and Mr. Treffingham—worse than useless! I have had some exasperating experiences with Mr. Treffingham, since he is my trustee as well as Almira's. Altogether he has taken great care for my own inheritance—but I cannot see him bringing a young girl out in London!"

At last Emma could see that Corinna had come around to her own way of thinking. She was seriously troubled. It was no small matter to bring a young lady into society, as Corinna knew herself, and even with the advantage of a much larger dowry than Almira could boast, one must be put in the way of meeting eligible young men.

"It is still early," Emma said, "and of course the child is still in mourning."

"She will be out of mourning before the new year," pointed out Corinna, "and if you are right about her perilous situation, it is not too early to take steps." She paused, then continued ruefully, "Only there is no place to start."

"Perhaps a husband can be found nearby—not Jack."

"You're thinking of Lady Hardie's brother?" exclaimed Corinna in a voice of unbelief. "I should not countenance any match with Mr. Willoughby!"

"Not even your own?" asked Emma, slyly. Mr. Willoughby, coming on a visit to his older sister, had apparently marked Corinna Darley for his own, and he was not easily discouraged.

Corinna chose to ignore Emma's teasing. "Of course it is not up to me to countenance, I am fully aware of that. But you, Emma, and I have some influence on her, and together—"

She stopped short. An odd expression passed over her features, and she smiled ruefully. "Do you know what I sound like? Lady Hardie herself. Emma dear, I beg you—do not let me become as hidebound in my ways as she is!"

Emma appeared distressed. "Corinna, I have not seen you so agitated before. I do think—" She too stopped short, and made a movement that in earlier times might have been described as girding up one's loins. "Well, then, it is time for serious talk from me, too. Corinna, I am far more worried about you than I ever would be about Almira. That child has the luck of a cat—always falling on her feet—and to worry about her is a lost cause. For a start, she pays no heed anyway."

"But how can you worry about me, Emma? I am not wealthy, of course, but my parents left me sufficient to get along."

Emma pursed her lips. Corinna was very dear to her, and she would not for the world hurt her, but some things needed to be said—as she deemed it— and the time seemed ripe.

"Not money. Husband."

"I don't need—"

Once launched, Emma brooked no interruption. "You want to waste your years away, taking the waters at Bath or Tunbridge Wells?"

"Hardly Tunbridge Wells," giggled Corinna. It was well known that one of the manifest benefits of a course of the waters there was an increase in fertility. "Although it helped poor Catherine of Aragon not at all!"

"Corinna," scolded Emma in mock severity, "that does not display a delicate mind."

"I don't think I have one," said Corinna frankly.

"You are trying to divert me," said Emma. "Of course I do not mean Mr. Willoughby. No one could be as desperate as to accept him. I have often thought—don't think me prying, my dear—but I have thought that there was someone particular that you fancied in those few months in London."

"No," said Corinna, too quickly. "Not—not at all!"

Emma did not dare to say more, at least on that subject. "But how," she resumed some moments later, "can you deal with the Hardie boy? Almira is perfectly capable of defying both of us, and short of locking her up, which I confess I should like to do, we cannot prevent her from meeting him secretly."

"I agree. But truly, I do not think there is cause for concern. He has an eye for the main chance, you know, or his mother does. I think it might be advisable to suggest to Lady Hardie that Almira's dowry is minuscule."

"Almira does have the duchess." Emma gave the title an English pronunciation, even though Maria Morland, Sir Rupert's only sister, now bore a French title—Duchesse de Carignac—courtesy of her third husband, now deceased.

"You have beguiled me," accused Corinna, "into forgetting what I wished to tell you. I have written the duchess."

Emma was startled out of her usual composure. "What did you say?"

"That it was her duty to launch her niece into society."

"And what did she answer?"

"Nothing. At least so far, she has not replied. But I think she must remember her duty. She has no one else, and Almira would make a far better match with the duchess's wealth in the offing. I know I sound indelicate, an eye out for the best chance for her, but you surely know that one look at Morland Hall in daylight would inform the most stupid suitor that there's no fortune here."

"And there would be only Jack Hardie left," added Emma. "Corinna, I had not thought you quite so enterprising."

"Someone has to be."

Later, alone, Corinna remembered one small observation Emma had made. *I have thought that there was someone particular that you fancied in those few months in London.* Emma's eyes were far too bright for Corinna's comfort. There had been indeed one particular gentleman—and he did not know Corinna existed.

She had not met him. She had seen him across the ballroom at Almacks's. He was taller than most other men, and his lean, sunburned features struck her fancy. She stared at him until her companion, a willowy young man of substantial means and little sense, noticed the direction of her gaze.

"*Farouche,* is he not? Name of Ferrington. Only heir to old Lonsdale. Something secret, but I understand very important, on the duke's staff in Spain. Home on leave, some injury, I collect. Can't think why any man of sense wants to go to the Peninsula. Mud and cannons and all. I suspect they do not even dine in a civilized fashion."

The tall man—Ferrington?—had moved away, and

she could see only the back of his head as he made his way toward a door leading to an inner room. She had thought for a moment—but she must have imagined it—that his eyes had locked with hers, and that some understanding, some strange intimacy, had passed between them. A fancy only, one that would have been dissolved had she been able to stay in London after that night, and perhaps met him and found that his feet were of clay.

But the next day she had been summoned home because of the grave illness of her mother, and London became merely a bright rainbow in her memory.

And so the man called Ferrington also had sunk into her memory, to surface once in a while in a dream, to be held privately and wistfully, as what might have been.

Instead of holding commerce with the tall Mr. Ferrington, she knew her fate, and her sense of loyalty to the stepfather who had been kind to her and whom her mother had loved was to be immured in this valley in Kent, with the burden of her young stepsister's care on her own slender shoulders.

It would have been more tolerable had Almira displayed any affection for those around her. The girl was possessed of a breathtaking beauty framed in shining black curls. It was no wonder that Jack found her alluring. At sixteen she had developed a figure which in coming years might well become buxom, and one must place hope in the possibility that her kittenish ways would in time be abandoned.

Her flawless beauty—the heart-shaped face, the long black lashes, the enticingly innocent smile—was stunning, if one did not notice the slight turndown at the corners of her full red lips, a sign of sullen selfishness that had come with the knowledge that she was thought to be a desirable female, and that she owned all of Morland Hall and was the sole mistress of the household staff. She did not quite dare to bring Emma under her thumb, and stood for the moment quite in awe of her older stepsister, Corinna, but the signs of future rebellion were clear to those who could read.

Morland Hall, on the outer facades, showed signs of decay. Almira was too self-centered to take steps toward repairing the fabric. She had too many schemes afoot to bother with what she considered insignificant details.

Her home would in a few years be falling to pieces around her, and she did not care.

CHAPTER 2

Nor were signs of neglect lacking inside the house. Later that morning, however, the two visitors to Morland Hall, just now seated in the salon, were oblivious to the sadly faded damask draperies and the shabby chair cushions, for they had more on their minds than dereliction of housekeeping.

Corinna Darley, sitting stiffly upright facing her visitors—unconsciously in an attitude of defiance—paid no heed to her surroundings, to which she was long accustomed. The three women could have been sitting in the unhealthy grotto of a gothic folly, for all she knew—or cared.

Anyone who knew her well—Emma Sanford, for example, or even her stepsister, Almira—would have discerned at once that Corinna was very angry indeed.

The vicar's wife, Mrs. Rumford, sat in a chair pulled up to the fireplace, in which a small fire struggled, and Lady Hardie, as became her greater consequence, sat in a massive chair previously sequestered to the use of the late Sir Rupert Morland. Lady Hardie filled the ample seat.

Corinna in the best of times dreaded the periodic visits of Lady Hardie, presented by the latter as the kindly visit of the premier lady of the neighborhood to inquire as to the well-being of the two orphans living in Morland Hall.

Lady Hardie took no notice of the fact that Corinna was all of twenty-three years old, nor that their financial affairs were in the tight and honest grip of trustees in London. Lady Hardie was capable of asking impertinent questions which she disguised as kindly interest.

"I vow," she would say, "it would be most unneighborly of me not to see how you children are making out. Such a sad state of affairs! I do not know how you endure, my dear Corinna."

Corinna's unspoken answer would have been along the lines of "Much better if you were to leave us alone," but being exceedingly well brought up, she desisted.

She was grateful at this moment for Almira's absence. Her young stepsister was much less courteous than she. Besides, Almira was more often than not the subject of Lady Hardie's most persistent inquiries.

But Corinna suspected that today's visitation by Lady Hardie carried overtones of an ominous nature. For one thing out of the ordinary, the vicar's wife today accompanied Lady Hardie, as though to bring to bear upon a sinner both the established church and the government, represented by proxy by Lady Hardie, whose husband's position as a justice of the peace bore little relation to his reputation as a wild man among the ladies.

Corinna, assessing the probabilities, wondered, "What has Almira done now?"

Mrs. Rumford glanced around her. "A wellproportioned room," she approved, "although sadly neglected. I have seldom been in this house. Sir Rupert, unlike the many other men of his station we have met, indeed have been in intimate congress with—they all of course had a very high opinion of Mr. Rumford—as I said, Sir Rupert did not

encourage Mr. Rumford's parochial visits to him."
She essayed a ladylike sniff.

Lady Hardie fixed her eyes on the corner of the
marble mantel. It was a mannerism that often moved
Corinna to unbecoming mirth. As though, she fancied, Lady Hardie were a basilisk who in great
kindness averted her deadly stare from her victims.
In line with this absurd fancy, Lady Hardie's voice
was gentle, but wounding.

"Perhaps," said Lady Hardie austerely, "it would
have been better if he had. I daresay Mr. Rumford
would have been of inestimable comfort to this
unfortunate household."

"But I do not consider us unfortunate," protested
Corinna, not for the first time, "save in the un-
timely deaths of my mother and stepfather."

"The vicar thinks," said Mrs. Rumford oppres-
sively, "that the plight of orphans is misery itself."

How tiresome! thought Corinna. She feared for a
moment that she had spoken aloud. However, the
expressions on the faces of the two ladies had not
altered, so Corinna breathed more easily. But she
resolved to guard her thoughts more rigidly.

"Is Miss Sanford still with you? I have not seen
her this long time," pursued the vicar's wife. "I do
hope she is still resident at Morland Hall. Young
ladies need a chaperon."

"In this case," Lady Hardie added, "one is quite
urgently needed. Where is she now?"

Emma Sanford was, Corinna had no doubt, cow-
ering upstairs in her room, fearing to be summoned
to the salon, and Corinna would have changed places
with her in a trice. "I really do not know," she said
aloud, in a dulcet tone. "I do not require her to
account to me every hour."

Mrs. Rumford drew a deep breath, preparing to

blast such impertinence out of existence. Lady Hardie hastily interrupted.

"Of course, she is Almira's companion, not yours. Although all would be solved if you were married. You did have a Season, did you not?"

And didn't take, thought Corinna honestly, except for an importunate young man with receding chin and wet palms, whose name she had forgotten. Although there was one man—

Mrs. Rumford paid little heed to Lady Hardie's well-intentioned interruption. She had a strong sense of injury, based on what she considered Sir Rupert's outrageous ignoring of her sainted husband. Her position in the community derived solely from her husband's position, since she herself was of indifferent birth and breeding. A slight to the vicar was a deep wound to her.

"Sir Rupert was sadly lacking in what was due to his consequence," she pronounced.

Corinna sprang to her late stepfather's defense. "I do not accept any criticism of Sir Rupert. He was exceedingly kind to me. He had no obligation to give me a home after my mother died."

Lady Hardie neatly inserted, "Spared him the expense of governesses and housekeepers, no doubt."

The vicar's wife protested, "You cannot mean that, Lady Hardie. You yourself informed me that Miss Sanford has been here for four years, in fact coming directly on the marriage of Sir Rupert and her mother." Carefully aiming her next arrow, she continued with an air of innocence, "Do you not remember? You told me you feared an early marriage between Miss Packer—one of the many governesses that Almira routed—and Sir Rupert. And Miss Packer was let go the instant that Lady Morland arrived."

Lady Hardie turned her basilisk stare directly on

her companion. "I do not recall ever saying anything quite so vulgar."

Mrs. Rumford retreated to gather her forces. This time, however, she turned to Corinna. "Lady Hardie is right. Your marriage, dear Miss Darley, would remove all questions of impropriety."

"Impropriety?" Corinna was by now beginning to suspect that there was indeed some undercurrent, some revelation yet to come, that would be at the least unpleasant, and possibly even a minor disaster.

She would have to speak to Almira herself, instead of letting Miss Sanford, whose position required her to monitor the behavior of young Miss Morland, point out the young lady's errors.

"A marriage, yes," said Lady Hardie repressively, "but a carefully arranged marriage, which would allow you to sponsor the child in a London Season."

Corinna's memory swept her back to that privately recollected face that stood out—in fact, the only vivid memory she retained—in her three months' stay in London, before she was recalled by the last illness of her mother.

Mentally erasing that face from her mind's eye, she inquired, trying for a light and inconsequent note, "Surely you have not called this morning to inform me that some gentleman has offered for me?"

Lady Hardie countered with a question of her own. "Surely you must know that my brother Clarence has been paying serious attention to you since he came to visit me? Although I do not urge his suit for him."

Mrs. Rumford murmured, "But that has naught to do with our purpose today."

"And," said Corinna in a quiet voice, "what is

your purpose today?" As though, she thought, she couldn't hazard a guess!

Mrs. Rumford flushed at what she considered the insolence in Corinna's voice. "This is just a social visit—" she began, but Lady Hardie was saying, "Actually, this is not a social visit—"

The two ladies exchanged a significant glance. By apparent consent, Lady Hardie spoke. "Dear child, I have been remiss. You have been much in need of guidance, and you did not call upon me. I had thought that in default of a relative of your own, you might have trusted me."

Corinna felt a wave of resentment sweep over her. Nettled, she lapsed into irony. "I assure you, I am grateful for your kind thoughts, even though—"

Mrs. Rumford interrupted. "Even though things would not be in this sad state, had we come earlier, even without an invitation."

As you did this time, thought Corinna.

The vicar's wife turned to Lady Hardie. "I *told* you—"

Lady Hardie quelled her with a look. Turning again to Corinna, she said, "Not to put too fine a point on it, Corinna, it's Almira. She's been riding out without a groom. Now, you know she's too old for that."

Emma's predictions came true for Corinna on the spot. All their shared fears about Almira's virtue, her headlong flight into trouble if not disgrace, took ugly shape with Lady Hardie's accusations. And neither Emma nor Corinna herself could stop her.

She felt a quaking somewhere inside—caused by dread, or anger, or more probably both. She could feel her cheeks warming, and hoped that her involuntary flush would not be taken as a sign of weakness. There was little she could do but to hear them out, for certainly she could not summon

Brixton to evict the vicar's wife as well as the first lady of the region. Her vivid fancy depicted for her the unseemly sight of Lady Hardie being thrust out of the entrance door onto the porch, in full sight of all the servants. The thought steadied her. Her lips twisted in an attempt to hide her sudden shaky amusement, and, thus fortified, she sprang to her stepsister's defense.

"She rides superbly," Corinna said. "I am no match for her, and of all things I do not wish to hold her back from the one enjoyment she has. I cannot believe she would come to harm on the estate, which is of course Morland land. And I am persuaded that she does not need to keep to Hyde Park custom here."

Lady Hardie pounced. "If she were riding in Hyde Park, I should like it better."

"I fail to see—"

"But I do. It was not precisely that she did not take her groom, but that she does not ride alone."

Corinna's heart sank at the heavy freight of disapproval invested in Lady Hardie's words.

"But—not alone?"

"Along the way," said Mrs. Rumford with an air of triumph, "she is joined by—a man!"

"A man?" echoed Corinna, bewildered.

"A man of little reputation, besides!"

Lady Hardie turned on the vicar's wife like a beast at bay. "Some idle gossip—made a mistake."

Corinna decided that innocence was the best defense. "You cannot mean—you surely do not refer to Jack?"

The expressions on the faces turned to her confessed the truth. "But they have grown up together! All her life he has known her!"

Mrs. Rumford, speaking Biblically, said, "Not yet perhaps."

Now that the point of their visit had been made, Lady Hardie grew expansive. "How foolish young people are! They do not see that constant companionship, propinquity, can lead them all unwitting into a situation that Almira cannot control."

Suddenly, in the blink of an eye, Corinna was furious. "Control? Why should Almira need to control any situation with Jack? Didn't you teach your son any decency?" She might have been warned by the lowering frowns on her callers, but she paid no heed. She realized now that what she was saying was quite unacceptable, and indeed she was sure that when she had time to reflect, she would be heartily ashamed of her diatribe. But she could not stop.

Like a stream in full spate, the words tumbled over each other. "Do you actually believe that your well-brought-up son, supposedly a gentleman, would so far give in to his baser feelings as to seduce a wellborn young lady of tender years?"

She was gratified to note the stunned expressions on the faces of her visitors. She had one more thing to ask—a devastating, very *vulgar* question.

"Or perhaps he takes after your husband?"

A dead silence ensued. Corinna watched, with some regret, as an embarrassed flush crept up Lady Hardie's heavy features. There seemed to be nothing to say. Corinna opened her lips to apologize, but thought better of it. No matter what she said, her apology could only worsen the situation.

But Mrs. Rumford, not at all sorry to see Lady Hardie discomfited, found her tongue. "You are too young to be aware of the grave danger to Almira."

Hotly, Corinna rounded on her new adversary. "If one cannot trust one's playfellow of years, then one cannot trust anyone. If Jack is such a rake, do you think the presence of a servant would stop him? For myself, I have never understood why the mere presence of a servant, whose position is certainly not one of authority and who is subject to dismissal in a moment, can be considered a deterrent to rakish behavior!"

With a reasonable air, Mrs. Rumford told her, "It is the talk, my dear, and servants let their tongues rattle on. One must not give them food for gossip—and that keeps the gentlemen in their places."

"I only hope you do not come too late to your senses," said Lady Hardie crossly. "You ought to be married at once. The situation here is too perilous—"

Scornfully, Corinna retorted, "You speak as though we were still in the Dark Ages, where lone females must be subject to the will of the nearest bully!"

Lady Hardie, now subdued, said, "Corinna, what we came for was to warn you, in the most kindly fashion, of a possible danger. Clearly, you do not choose to listen. You should, may I point out, be grateful for our concern, since you have no female relatives to take an interest in you."

Corinna, ashamed of her previous outburst, grasped the olive branch. "You forget Almira's aunt. The Duchesse de Carignac."

"Ah, my child, of course. An impressive connection. But is she here? Does she take a daily interest? Do not try to fob me off, Corinna. The duchess is doubtless in France at this moment."

Actually, as Corinna did not know, the duchess was in Vienna, hoping to negotiate with Napoleon's conquerors and reclaim her husband's vast French estates. Her letter to Almira's aunt had been forwarded, and forwarded again, thus delayed by weeks.

So far, the duchess had evinced little interest in her niece. In truth, she had not even responded when Almira wrote to her—under coercion—to inform her of Sir Rupert's fatal accident.

This situation Corinna was not disposed to share with her inquisitors. Still heated by the embers of anger, she became reckless. "Of course she takes an interest in Almira. In truth, we had a letter only this past sennight."

It was not a falsehood. She did not explain that the letter in question came from a distant cousin of Corinna's, begging for monetary help in her distress.

Corinna rose. "Believe me, I understand your concern. It would not suit me in the least for Almira to develop a *tendre* for your son." For emphasis, she added, "Not in the least!"

Let Jack's mother make what she would of that!

But Lady Hardie, on her way out, had the last word, pronounced with the gravity commonly attributed to the Delphic oracle.

"That young minx will bring you nothing but trouble until she finds her master! And, Corinna, I must tell you that I will have a word with my brother. I should not wish to see him wed to a woman so stubborn, so headstrong, as not to listen to words of advice given to her only for her own good. Nor will I scruple to tell him that your stepsister is in a fair way to lose her reputation, for no matter what happens, I will not allow Jack to marry her."

"Nor will I consent!" flared Corinna.

"Do not count on my brother's offering for you! I will do my best to discourage him."

"Pray do," recommended Corinna enthusiastically. "I should be grateful."

Mrs. Rumford, with a burst of shrewdness, murmured, "How very proper of you, Lady Hardie, not to lend your support to Mr. Willoughby's suit. No matter how comfortable her fortune is."

Lady Hardie favored the vicar's wife with a look

containing daggers, and stumped out of the room, and out to her carriage.

On the entrance porch, Corinna watched the carriage until it was out of sight down the drive. She could sustain with fortitude the thought that they would not call again for at least a fortnight. She sighed, and went into the house.

CHAPTER 3

From her bedroom window on an upper floor, Emma Sanford watched the carriage containing the two visitors until it was out of sight beyond the first curve in the drive.

Only then did she consider it safe to emerge to go to Corinna's assistance. She knew full well that any blame attached to this household, deemed rudderless after the death of Sir Rupert, would devolve upon her bowed shoulders. When one is well bred enough to remember past prosperity, and is only too conscious of one's present lowly state—chaperon to an ungrateful child without rosy prospects—one instinctively seeks preservation as the primary guiding rule.

Emma knew well enough that dear Corinna needed no support. She was not lacking in presence, and could well deal with impertinence in a suitably quelling manner. Emma, consequently, descended the stairs and entered the main salon with never the slightest suspicion of matters gone awry.

She was therefore stunned almost to speechlessness at the first words hurled at her by her dear Corinna.

"I am not fit company, Emma, and I advise you to depart in haste—before I give way to strong hysterics!"

"Corinna!"

"I am excessively angry—I have never encountered such presumption! Do you tell Brixton—or I will, with pleasure—that I am not at home. Neither to Mr. Willoughby, should he chance to call, nor to those—those—"

Emma, seeing that Corinna could not find words, murmured, "Not at home to the vicar's wife? Surely not! Or Lady Hardie? Dear Corinna, do reconsider! It will not do to turn hermit!"

"Do not try to tell me they did not mean to insult me, for I shall not believe it. I will not receive those harridans in my house ever again!"

Emma did not believe the present moment a proper time to point out that Morland Hall was not Corinna's house. She essayed a soothing, "Now, Corinna—" But it was as useless as speaking into the wind.

"Do you know what they had the effrontery—the unmitigated arrogance!—the—the—" Corinna took a turn around the room. "They said that Almira must not see any more of Jack Hardie!"

Emma said with relief, "Then this solves the problem."

Corinna stormed on, not heeding Emma's pacific comment, "Lest *she* lead *him* astray, if you can credit such idiocy!"

Emma mused, "I wonder how they thought we might accomplish such a separation."

"You must be mistaken, Emma! The two of them have been neighbors since childhood! He could not entertain thoughts of taking advantage of Almira. He has always been most kind to her, like the older brother she considers him, I warrant you!"

"But Almira is growing into a great beauty, dear Corinna—I should not be surprised were he to consider her in a new light—we have been so distracted by Sir Rupert's accident that we have

scarcely noticed—and she resents any restrictions—"
Emma, at least that day, was not destined to finish
a sentence.

"How dare Lady Hardie tell me that if my sister
is seduced it is my fault? I ask you—hasn't that
woman taught her son any of the decencies?"

Emma took refuge in a literal response. "Don't
ask me, my dear. You should have asked Lady
Hardie."

Corinna stopped short. Amusement was never
far beneath the surface with her, and now she suddenly grinned. She looked at that moment, thought
her doting Emma, about sixteen years old instead
of the twenty-three she was.

"I did. That was when they took their precipitate
departure." She thought a moment. "If I had known
such a remark would speed them on their way, I
should have found occasion to use it earlier."

"I wish I had heard you. It would have been such
a treat!"

Corinna dropped into a chair and folded her hands
in her lap. "Oh dear, Emma. Have I done such a
dreadful thing? I did rant a bit, I'm afraid. But
they did upset me!"

"Was that their complaint? That Almira and
Jack—?"

"That was the only new thing," Corinna informed
her. "The constant theme of Lady Hardie, you know,
is that we should not live here alone. And I should
marry. And what was Sir Rupert thinking of?" She
frowned. "What she thinks I have to say on this
head, I cannot decipher. It was none of my doing
that Sir Rupert flung himself and his stallion over
the gate, in that idiotic fashion. He knew full well
that Thundercloud hated to jump."

Emma made soothing sounds, but Corinna, wrapped in her indignation, ignored her.

"If he had time," Corinna continued, a wistful note creeping into her voice, "he would have made arrangements, I am sure of it. He was so good to me, letting me stay after my mother died, that I cannot abandon his daughter, no matter how little she regards me. Nor can I desert you, dear Emma. But I do wish Lady Hardie would not come bleating around, like an old sheep."

Emma laughed. "Corinna, I despair of you!"

"Oh, please don't, Emma. Without you I cannot imagine how we would go on."

Emma had an uneasy thought of her own. "I suppose Lady Hardie, or Mrs. Rumford, suggested that I was not up to the position of chaperon?"

"No, but they did think at first I would be well advised to accept Mr. Willoughby."

Emma, encouraged by Corinna's return to a semblance of her usual good humor, inquired, "And will you?"

"Do you know, I think I have whistled him down the wind. Lady Hardie will not encourage dear Clarence to offer for a stubborn ape-leader."

"She did not call you that!" exclaimed Emma, shocked.

"Not quite. But it will be a day to mark well—the day I listen to either of those old—"

"Corinna!" warned Emma automatically.

The two sat in silence for a few moments. Corinna reflected, somewhat more calmly than before, on the gist of the visitors' remarks. Truly, the situation of Corinna Darley, and the very young and inexperienced Miss Almira Morland, was far from satisfactory.

All of Sir Rupert's modest fortune was entangled in a trust for the benefit of his daughter. Corinna, being no relation to the Morlands, had no say in the matter of the trust. She had through her mother, whose happy second marriage to Sir Rupert had been of short duration, a modest competence, and from her father's will, a more than adequate fortune. But there was no one of Almira's relation able to bring the girl out into society.

There was, as she and Emma had discussed only that morning, Almira's Aunt Maria, who had first married an untitled gentleman whose name Corinna, coming late into the family, had never heard, then Sir Percy Somebody, before taking for her third husband the French aristocrat Etienne de Carignac, who had sought refuge in England during the tumultuous days of the French Revolution. Aunt Maria had outlived the duke, to her sorrow, for she had expected to reclaim the vast ducal acres in the fruitful Loire Valley when Napoleon had been put in his place, a happy event that had taken place only last May.

But unless Aunt Maria took steps, there was little expectation of a London Season for Almira, and less chance of an advantageous marriage.

Emma, as though following Corinna's mental tracks, said, "Where is the duchess?"

"I haven't any idea whatever. Nor, to be truthful, do I care, since she has not had the courtesy to reply to me. Emma, I told Lady Hardie the most shocking lie! I told her we had a letter from her last week!"

"Corinna! You did not!" exclaimed Emma, but her tone was indulgent. "Perhaps she will yet take an interest in her great-niece."

"I think not. It has been two months since I wrote. And of course she was informed when Sir Rupert died, but we heard nothing from her then, either. There was a rift, you know—although I had not realized it was so serious. But of all things, I can barely sustain the thought of dealing further with the duchess. Lady Hardie is quite sufficient for me, thank you."

"I confess I think the vicar's wife is quite beyond everything."

"I think—I think I shall simply vanish, leave Morland Hall, and let the trustees deal with Lady Hardie."

"Where will you go, my dear?" asked Emma in a most practical voice. "I shall wish to know your direction."

Catching a glimpse of Emma's expression, Corinna chuckled. "You tricked me into seeing how silly I am! Not a sign of shock! I wonder, dear Emma— what would have the power to shock you?"

Seeing that Corinna had returned to her normal good nature, Emma Sanford allowed herself to consider the question seriously. "What would shock me?" she echoed. "I cannot imagine, for you, my dear, have such enormous good sense—"

Corinna pounced. "A certain note in your voice leads me to wonder—you have reservations, Emma. Now then, out with it!"

"Slang does not add to a young lady's charm," said Emma severely, but automatically. She flushed. "Well, it would perhaps *surprise* me, rather than shock. But I confess to a *wee* desire to see you lose your wits—"

"Now you shock me!"

"Oh, not disastrously, my dear," countered Emma with a smile. "But if you were to tumble into it—a great love, for example—and just once be head over heels foolish—" Emma subsided in pink confusion.

Corinna said severely, "I would consider any such eventuality as quite beyond the realm of possibility. Oh dear, I do sound pompous, do I not?"

"My dear Corinna—please believe me. I had no desire—I should not have spoken so."

"Nothing to forgive. If I had ever been suscepti-ble to such a brainstorm, it would have happened long since. Now that I have reached the great age of three-and-twenty, I am persuaded that such a state of mind would be uncomfortable in the extreme."

Corinna refused to be cast down over the mo-mentary loss, so to speak, of Mr. Willoughby. He had proved himself persistent, and she did not doubt his eventual return to her company.

The danger lay in the possibility that she might welcome him! The lot of an unmarried woman, unless she was wealthy enough to be eccentric, and courted for her favors, was drab at best. More than one woman took an unattractive husband to avoid such a fate.

She was determined that she would never suc-cumb to such a temptation. However, it might be well to fix firmly in one's mind the fate that might once have been hers. Deliberately she allowed her thoughts once again to focus on a certain face that had begun to fade in her memory.

She had believed that she had put Justin Ferring-ton—now, she knew, become Lord Lonsdale on the death of an aged relative—out of her mind for good. After all, she told herself severely, there was noth-ing to remember. To be reminded of him thrice in one day was so unlikely as to rouse her suspicions. Was she bordering on an obsession with a phan-tom? After all, the last and only time she had seen him was two years since.

Except that recollection did not agree.

That naughty jade Memory perversely was able to bring up the features of Lord Lonsdale as pre-cisely, as three-dimensionally, as though he stood facing her in this very room.

He was well above the average height, but did

not appear so because of the breadth of his muscled chest. His sunburned skin and an unusual blond streak in his dark hair spoke of outdoor living in an area where the sun shines hotter than in England. His rugged jaw and direct compelling gaze etched him indelibly on her mind.

But in addition to the clear details of his features, there was a strong impression of power, of authority. And just at the moment, Corinna longed for the comfort, the security, of someone who might take charge of her life. Only for a while, though—but how nice it would be to lean on a hard-muscled chest, feel strong arms around her—like a rampart, ephemeral though it might be, against her own weakness.

She came to herself with a start. How silly she was! But a dark suspicion crept into her mind. That night, two years ago, she had felt a fluttering uneasiness as his eyes held her gaze. It was a kind of trepidation that originated somewhere near her stomach and moved stealthily into her limbs, making her knees weak. For the first time, she wondered—would this be the kind of sensation that Emma Sanford had mentioned? A mad, head-over-heels fluttering?

Try as she might, for the sake of experiment, to summon up that same sensation, she could not. Her common sense returned. One glimpse two years before—she would have to be mad indeed to cling to such a memory. Although, to be honest, she added to herself, there was nothing else to cling to!

Aloud, as though to impress the thought doubly on her mind, she told herself, "Almira produces enough gothic emotion in a day to last us both for six months!"

CHAPTER 4

Before Corinna descended too deeply into the swamp of self-pity, she was interrupted by the return to the house of her stepsister.

Corinna gazed at Almira with abstract pleasure. She was growing, as Emma had pointed out, from an awkward child into a lissome beauty, one capable of cutting a wide swath through the drawing rooms of London, leaving eligible young men swooning in her wake. Such a waste! she thought. Every woman knew she must be happier wed than unwed—this was a fact of life.

Corinna was prone to amuse herself by recalling apposite poetry, sometimes a bit antiquated, since much of her education had been garnered by voracious reading in Sir Rupert's neglected library.

Now a poetic phrase sprang unbidden to her mind: "To waste its sweetness on the desert air." Not that this valley in Kent was a desert—far from it as far as flora and fauna went. But there was a distinct drought of possible husbands on the horizon. That is, if one did not count Jack Hardie—and Corinna did not.

One glance at the girl's face, wind-whipped to a rosy color that admirably complemented her dark curls, told Corinna that something of an untoward nature had occurred. Had Jack overstepped the bounds of decency? She could not believe it.

She forced her voice to an equable note. "Have a good ride?"

"Oh, yes, Corinna, we did. You know, quite by chance I met Jack and we went all the way to the village, and beyond. Do you know that from the top of Penshill . . ." Her voice died away. Penshill was far beyond the boundaries of the Morland estate, as Corinna now pointed out to her erring stepsister.

"My dear, I have often defended you to Lady Hardie by telling her that you never rode beyond your own farms. Now you tell me quite different. Even as far as Penshill? That must be all of five miles away! You did say you were with Jack quite by chance?"

"You do not believe me?"

"You really could not expect me to swallow such a bouncer! Truly, Almira, how can you rate me such a lackwit?" Her tone was half humorous, and Almira was led into further confidences.

"Well, then, only partly by chance."

"And you of course did not take Fox with you? Almira, I cannot think how you can be so careless of your reputation. Certainly it is not for lack of knowing how to go on."

"You don't trust me!" Almira wailed.

"I have, until now. But you will recall that you assured me that you always observed the conventions when away from Morland Hall, and I did not question you."

"Jack takes care of me. You cannot think ill of him!"

"I should be most reluctant to do so. But it appears that he has given little thought to protecting you from gossip."

"Oh, but he has! You cannot think harshly of him when you hear what he wants me to do. You would never guess!" Corinna agreed, although si-

lently she wondered what Almira would say if
Corinna came out with the bald suggestion that
Jack Hardie had seduced her.

"Wants you to do what?" Her stepsister fell silent. Corinna's heart sank to the toes of her worn
slippers. "You had best tell me, Almira," she continued, "for I must tell you that I have had visitors
this morning."

Almira found speech. "Miss Sanford told me,"
she exclaimed tragically. "You aren't going to listen
to those old—"

"Almira!" warned Corinna.

Abashed only for the moment, Almira said, "But
you know they are—old witches!"

Corinna leaned back in her chair and frowned at
her stepsister, no longer amused. The girl's father
had spoiled her inordinately, and died suddenly,
leaving the result of his doting to Corinna to deal
with. Unfortunately, thought Corinna, her character had not kept pace with her outward attributes.
Always impulsive, and prone to throw articles,
sometimes of value, when her temper was roused,
she was as easily swayed as a weathercock, always
reflecting the thoughts of her most recent companion.

Emma more than once had reassured Corinna on
this head. "She is too young and inexperienced, my
dear. She will grow out of this phase when she
meets someone with a steady mind."

Corinna quirked an eyebrow. "And if she doesn't?"

"God help us all," said Emma fervently, "to live
through the scandal!"

But such a happy prospect as a gentleman with a
steady mind had not appeared, as yet, and Corinna
was not optimistic as to the future. She had no
means at hand of providing Almira with the de-
sired husband.

Cooler now than when her visitors had been with her, Corinna began to suspect that there might be some truth in their accusations.

"Almira, you did not answer me. What does Jack Hardie want you to do?"

Knowing Almira so well, Corinna could almost see decision being made behind her lovely innocent eyes. Corinna braced herself to sustain without shock Almira's explanation. The girl hesitated a moment too long, and Corinna was instantly persuaded she was not about to hear the truth.

"He simply wants me to go with him to the Assembly in Wrotham. I know I'm in mourning, but surely—only six weeks yet, and I could wear my purple silk—and you could lend me your black cashmere shawl—"

Dryly, Corinna broke into the rhapsody. "If I lend you my shawl, then what would I wear to the Assembly?"

"Oh!" It was clear that Almira had not expected Corinna to make one of Jack's projected party. "Would *you* want to go? It will be all young people, you know!"

An unintended insult, Corinna thought, but nonetheless painful for that. "I would of course accompany you, as would Emma. How could you have thought otherwise? But I think we must refuse. It does not look well to skimp your year of mourning."

Almira thrust out her lower lip mutinously. "Well, Jack said you would not let me go."

"At least he has some sense."

Almira considered a moment. Then, in a burst, she said, "Then I'm glad I did what else he asked me to. I wrote to Aunt Maria!"

Of all the things Corinna might have expected to hear, this suggestion was not even on her mental list. "You wrote—for Jack? To the duchess? When did you write? I did not think he was acquainted with her. Why on earth would he want you to write to her?"

The sheer outrageousness of this development convinced Corinna that Almira was telling the truth, this time.

"She is very rich, is she not?"

Quellingly, Corinna said, "I have not the slightest idea. Nor is it considered the thing to speculate on the subject." Then, curiosity getting the better of her, she asked, "Why do you wish to know?"

"She's our only hope!"

"Hope for what?" Corinna asked, dreading the answer.

"For m-my d-dowry!"

Corinna required a long moment to adjust her thoughts. Somehow they had gotten quite out of focus. "Dowry?" she echoed at last, in a reasonably calm voice. "Then—are you telling me that all is settled between you and Jack—and I must presume also with Mr. Treffingham? It is customary, you know, to consult with one's trustee—"

"You're angry. I knew you would be."

"You might well have expected it. You know, Almira, there is sufficient money set aside—so Mr. Treffingham told us—for an adequate dowry for a suitable marriage. And even for a modest Season. The question is whom to ask to sponsor you." As an afterthought, she added, "I suppose I must point out that any arrangements must wait until you are out of mourning. And even Jack would not try to marry you before you are of age, without Mr. Treffingham's approval."

"There's nobody to sponsor me. Except Aunt Maria. I'm glad I wrote. And Jack says . . ."

"What did Jack say?"

"You wouldn't understand."

"Try me," recommended Corinna. Almira's ingenuous expression told Corinna more than she wished to know. Suspicion prodded her. Good God, how far had the child gone?

She did not realize she had spoken aloud until Almira answered, literally. "I told you. To Penshill."

With a dignity so new it sat awkwardly on her shoulders, Almira continued, "Perhaps Jack is not the best husband for me. But I don't know anybody else—and I *hate* living here and going nowhere and Emma and you always scolding me. And it is my house now, and Jack says I could make you both leave—and I wrote to Aunt Maria last month, and I should hear any day now."

"But my dear—"

Almira's voice began to rise, always a danger sign. "And Jack says he'll take me to London but my dowry is not enough, because he does not want to live in *poverty* and neither do I—"

"Almira!" The sharp note in Corinna's voice brought the girl up short—and gave Corinna time to think. Jack was indeed revealing himself to be not above seducing a female of Almira's breeding. For a few moments, her imagination ran riot along lines she could only consider as vulgar. But she needed to know exactly where Almira stood—or, heaven forbid, had lain. "Did he—did he touch you?"

Unable to hide a quick start of guilt, Almira tugged at her sleeve, but not in time to conceal from Corinna a dark red welt on her wrist.

"How can you understand, Corinna? You've never been in love. Nor ever will be! I hate you!"

Almira rushed out of the room, leaving the door open behind her. Corinna could hear the uninhibited sounds of racking sobs diminishing in the distance up the stairs. She had no doubt that the servants had missed nothing of Almira's state of mind.

Her own state of mind was sufficiently agitated that she felt the need of fresh air, preferably blowing a gale through her mind and carrying away everything she had heard in the last hour. She went upstairs in search of a warm cloak, stopping in Emma Sanford's room.

Emma's bedroom adjoined her charge's, and the sounds of an ungoverned temper relieving itself in mild hysterics penetrated the wall between. Emma whispered, "What happened? I told her about Lady Hardie's visit—I thought it would make it easier for you if she knew before she came to you. Was that a mistake?"

"No matter. We would be diverted by just such a display whenever she found out. No, Emma, I must tell you what maggot Jack Hardie has put in her mind." She proceeded to inform Emma. "And I think he did touch her—but not in *that* way. Only hurt her wrist, I gather. I don't like it, Emma. There is violence in him, and I never suspected it. Perhaps you—"

"I will try." Emma frowned. "It is not right that you should have to deal with this—this ill-tempered brat. She is no relation of yours."

"I owed Sir Rupert much. May I leave Almira with you? I think a walk might serve to cool my own passion. I imagine you would not like to deal with two of us throwing tantrums and vases all about?"

Emma watched her leave with as strong an emotion as either of her companions might have displayed. Emma's feelings, however, ran along the lines of great distress over the unpleasant situation of Corinna, and a compelling wish to box young

Almira's ears for her. She listened for some time to the dwindling sounds from the next room. Calculating to a nicety the moment when her entrance might be most effective, she rose to the call of duty and entered young Almira's bedroom.

CHAPTER 5

The air was not only fresh, but unusually cold for the middle of November, and Corinna walked quickly. Today's scene with Lady Hardie and her colleague was, to say the least, distressing. Almira's subsequent behavior had only exacerbated Corinna's concern and added to her growing suspicions.

The old fairy-tale dictum "What I tell you three times is true" lurked in her mind and darkened her thoughts. She had certainly been informed more than thrice that Almira was in a fair way to lose her untouched reputation.

Suspicion grew—fed by reflection on Lady Hardie's strong representations—into a kind of fear. It was all well and good to protest that any intrigue or seduction must be laid at young Jack Hardie's door. And intrigue there was, according to Almira, even though Corinna was not prepared—quite—to believe seduction.

Her step abruptly slowed. Seduced? In all likelihood, no. But there was certainly a hint of covert intimacy between the two. See how Jack had suggested that Almira might rid herself of the two ladies in her household!

Further indications that Jack was taking far too intrusive an interest in Almira was his suggestion that she write to her aunt and ask not for her help

in presenting Almira to society but—so it seemed—
for money! And the silly goose had written!

Playfellows, Corinna had called them to Lady
Hardie, somewhat inaccurately—more like brother
and sister was what she meant. But doubt assailed
her—there was something newly awry with her
understanding of the situation.

Was it possible that Almira had fallen in love
with Jack Hardie? Impossible to accept! And,
thought Corinna, equally impossible to deal with.
She began to realize the full extent of her helpless-
ness. She had no authority over Almira—not by
blood, not by law. She could even be thrown out of
Morland Hall, the only home she knew! And yet
the girl must be brought out in London, and an
advantageous marriage arranged for her—and who
was to make such vital arrangements?

Although Corinna's blood cooled with the slower
pace she had set, her brain seemed to heat up to
provide solutions, none of which answered the problem. Sir Rupert had left everything he possessed in
a trust for Almira, in the hands of two antiquated
and aristocratic trustees, and Mr. Treffingham. No
help there in launching Almira into society.

Nor had Corinna any family on whom she could
call, even in desperation. The only person in the
world who might feel an obligation to sponsor Almira
was her aunt the duchess, and Corinna considered
that lady a frail reed indeed. The Duc de Carignac,
a charming aristocrat whose fortune had fallen vic-
tim to the Bonaparte regime, had died more than a
year ago, not living long enough to know of Bonaparte's defeat and his exile to Elba. Aunt Maria's
indignation knew no bounds when she realized that
her husband had died too soon to reclaim his French
estates. Sir Rupert had told her, when she attempted
to enlist his help in their recovery, that she was

greedy. She had retorted that he was a lackwit who soon would be pockets to let. The relationship had suffered, and the duchess had not even come to her brother's funeral.

No help there, thought Corinna.

Away from Almira, she felt more patient with the girl. Almira was bereft of her doting father, and it was no wonder she sought for some kind of affection. She could be beguiling as a kitten, and had been for the most part a loving affectionate child. But now she seemed to resent everything around her. One could not point out the slightest need for correction without running the real danger of becoming a target for a thrown book, or, for that matter, even china if it was at hand.

Child was the accurate term, thought Corinna.

What could she ever do? Almira must not be allowed to become infatuated with Jack Hardie. Corinna had a dark suspicion that perhaps she was already too late. But possibly, if she did not object too strongly, Almira would forget her *tendre* for him. There had been others before Jack—Corinna remembered vividly a dreadful three weeks when Almira was bent on marrying the curate and traveling to Africa as a missionary. Sir Rupert's wrath was formidable—and Almira came by her own temper honestly.

Ahead of her lay a gap in the boundary hedge, giving passage onto Hardie lands. Idly, Corinna walked through, and stood at the edge of the fallow field.

At the far end of the field moved a lone rider, whom she did not at first recognize. But when he turned his horse and saw her, and came at a gallop across the field toward her, she knew him. Jack was obviously coming to meet her, and she stayed where she was and waited.

When he drew near, he reined up. "Oh, it's you, Corinna," he said in a tone that seemed to mean, "How dare you pretend to be someone else, when I expected Almira?"

"Yes, Jack. It's not a pleasant day for a walk," she added almost apologetically, "but I needed the fresh air."

He nodded absently. "You didn't come to ring a peal over me, then?"

"Why should I? Oh, I collect you mean that excursion to Wrotham. You must have known she could not go."

He grinned. "I was sure that you would not let her go, but she was determined on the project. She insisted that she wanted to go and I must take her."

"So you let me give her the bad news?" Corinna quizzed.

"Better to have her angry with you than me, don't you agree?"

"No, I don't!"

He laughed, a harsh sound on the gusting wind. "She is thoroughly and constantly angry with you, Corinna. You have nothing to lose."

With narrowed eyes, Corinna repeated, "Lose?"

"Well, I did not mean exactly lose," he said awkwardly. "But she is bound to be angry with you and Miss Sanford, no matter what you do."

Since when have you become an expert on Almira's vagaries? she wondered, but was relieved to find she had not spoken aloud.

"And you do not help in the least!" she told him. "Filling her head with ideas that I cannot approve of! Now she's talking about getting rid of Emma— and me—and how can she possibly go on in that fashion, without anyone to lend her countenance? It's fustian!"

Jack's first answer was a broad grin. "Corinna,

you never did know how to handle her. You're as different as cheese and chalk!"

Jack, no doubt with the kindest motives, continued to confide in Corinna as though they were old friends. Ordinarily she considered him crude and heavy-handed at best, but for a moment he was unexpectedly shrewd in his advice. "She is growing up, you know. I remember how it was with me, angry at everything, feeling hedged in all the time, not enough money to break away from all this—"

Corinna did not answer, for there was nothing she could think of to say, except to warn him about laying violent hands on Almira. But she did not *know* that he was to blame for the welt on her wrist. After a moment, Jack changed the subject. "I hope you hear good news of the duchess?"

Corinna looked up swiftly. "It is odd that you should ask, for your mother inquired only this morning."

Jack seemed to stiffen in his saddle. He was a stockily built young man, giving an impression not of honesty but of undisciplined force, as though he claimed the right to ride roughshod over any opponent.

The sky had darkened to a slate gray, and the wind rose, lifting dead leaves and sending them into small eddies around her ankles. In the lessened light, Jack's features blurred in her vision. The figure rose in the saddle, and for an instant as she looked up at him, she was aware of the most unpleasant feeling—almost a sense of fear. Nonsense! she told herself firmly. It's only Jack!

As though he thought he had talked too freely to her, he swung his steed around and galloped off without even a civil leavetaking. Ruefully, she conceded that he did touch his whip to his cap! She watched horse and rider out of sight. Still she lingered in the gap, reflecting on the odd encounter. *I didn't ask him to tell me anything,* she pointed out in her mind. *And what presumption he has to tell me what kind of girl Almira is!*

All in all, she thought, Jack had changed while she was not looking, much as Almira had changed. She had seen him often enough, of course, but always as Almira's friend. Now she saw him as a grown man of mature years, but possibly juvenile understanding. If Jack had meant to reassure her, he had failed. She was more unquiet in her mind than ever.

Back on the Morland side of the hedge, Corinna turned to walk along the hedge until she reached the limit of the field. A stile provided access to the public road that bordered that field, and Corinna climbed to sit on the top step. She was not ready to return to the clamorous stuffiness of Morland Hall. She thought wryly that the time might come when she would long to be safe at Morland Hall—after Almira had evicted her!

Corinna did not know how long she perched on the top step of the stile, huddled in her warm cloak, the cold wind swirling around her. What would she do, she wondered, if Almira were no longer her responsibility?

She had a more than adequate competence of her own, inherited from her own parents, and she was therefore independent, even if not wildly prosperous. Would she go to Bath—and become a withered spinster whose days revolved around the gossip of the Pump Room? Never.

She would travel—

But all the possibilities that came to her fell upon barren ground. She knew she had lost all chance of an acceptable marriage when her mother had fallen ill and she was summoned home. She

could tell herself as firmly as possible that if anyone had wished to see more of her, he would have
found a way to seek her out. Certainly the man
whose features she remembered so well—the man
with such an air of power and authority—would
have found no difficulty in tracing her, had he been
interested.

And firmly, yet again, she recognized that dreaming of Justin Ferrington was the most futile exer-
cise of imagination one could think of.

Much better—if she was to indulge her taste for
fantasy!—to think about what she could do for
Almira. She would write to the trustees—she would
write again to Aunt Maria—she might be forced to
forbid Jack Hardie entry to the house, bar the doors,
put a shotgun in old Brixton's shaky hands—

But her wildest fantasy could not have encompassed the strange occurrence that was only moments away.

The wind had grown to stronger gusts, and there
was more than a hint of ice in it. The little gusts
toyed with the hem of her cloak, and she tucked
the border between her small boot and the step of
the stile, to hold it close.

From far away in the direction of the village,
riding on the fitful wind, came the sound of hoof-
beats. Under the windswept sky, shivering with
cold, she could almost believe it was a fateful sound.
Someone was coming, and at this moment there
was no one Corinna cared to meet.

The sound of hooves was intriguing, and she listened with the expert knowledge of a countrywoman.
Not the heavy clopping sound of draft horses, nor
the intermittent squeak of ill-oiled wagon wheels.
Who then? Lady Hardie would not return for at
least a week, allowing time for her sensibilities to

recover, and Jack was behind her in the field beyond the hedge.

A stranger, then? Someone to avoid?

Particularly did she wish to avoid being seen sitting on a stile in the midst of an oncoming November storm. What credit she had would suffer from such a tale!

But she did not have time to move, to say nothing of retreating behind a hedge, out of sight. The oncoming vehicle was, as soon as she caught sight of it, recognizable as being something quite out of the ordinary. A curricle drawn by a pair of splendid matched blacks grew larger as it neared, and she sat unmoving on the stile, fascinated by the smart vehicle. To her astonishment, the curricle drew up opposite the stile. There were two men in the vehicle, obscured to her vision by the shadow of the hood.

"Pray tell me," asked the man holding the reins, a gentleman by his voice, "am I right for Morland Hall?"

"M-Morland Hall!" Her voice came stuttering her surprise. "What do you want at Morland Hall?"

"Simply the directions. Is that exceptionally difficult?"

"No, not at all, sir. But I cannot understand—" An emissary from Mr. Treffingham? That was the only possibility she could envision of persons of this quality having business at Morland Hall. "Are you from London?"

Hastily, she wished the words unspoken. What must he think of her, sitting inelegantly on a stile and demanding to know his business!

The pleasant voice came again from the dusky interior of the curricle, very coolly, in a most daunting tone. "Where I come from is not in the least the subject of discussion here, nor is it any of your affair."

"But—I—"

"I apologize for disturbing you," he interrupted ruthlessly. "We will seek directions from someone else, more civil perhaps."

She took a deep breath. Did he think her a country maid to be spoken to in such fashion?

"I should deem it unlikely," she said with enormous dignity, "that you would understand the uses of civility were they standing before you."

A gleam of white teeth in the dusk told her the gentleman, whoever he was, was amused. "A proper setdown, but—"

In her turn she interrupted. "You are right for Morland Hall. The gates are a scant half mile ahead of you."

She loosened her cloak from one foot where she had held it fast against the wind and made to get to her feet, to have at least the advantage of standing upright.

She moved, as usual, too quickly. One foot was still wrapped in the folds of the velvet cloak, and she scrabbled to gain her balance. She had sat too long in the chilling air.

Instead of the graceful descent she intended from her urchin's perch, her limbs betrayed her and she sprawled headlong on the ground.

Above her she heard an indistinct exclamation— sounding very much like a muttered curse, with which she agreed wholeheartedly—and the noise of quick footsteps on the road.

"My apologies," said the deep voice which had first addressed her. "I should not have startled you so."

The owner of the pleasant voice knelt beside her on the ground and helped her sit up.

"My cloak," Corinna began.

"Has taken no harm, I believe." An altered note crept into his voice as he realized the quality of her attire, and therefore the quality of the young lady he supported with his arm.

"Oh, what a fool I am!" groaned Corinna.

"Not at all," said her rescuer civilly.

She looked up into his face, and thought for a moment the world had altered from reality to fantasy.

She was—and even in a mad dream she would not have conjured up such a situation as this!—half lying on the frozen ground, held in the arms of— she could *not* be mistaken!—the arms of Justin Ferrington, Lord Lonsdale.

CHAPTER 6

Earlier in that autumn of 1814, in the city of Vienna, Lord Lonsdale drained the last drop of chocolate from a fine porcelain cup and set it down on the breakfast table. He regarded the cup thoughtfully without truly seeing it, and let his gaze wander around the room, noting with approval the tiled fireplace in which a small but vigorous fire burned, and the two comfortable chairs drawn up to it.

Rather less than a year ago, he had been with Wellington, entering France over the snowy Pyrenees from the Peninsula, riding north to tree Bonaparte outside of Paris.

The Peninsular Wars had been many things to many people. For the Ferringtons—both Justin and his cousin Francis—it had been dreary, bone-chilling cold, exhausting heat, and no respite from the danger of a sniper bullet or an unexpected betrayal by an informer.

Wellington relied for information about the enemy—the French army—on a number of intelligence gatherers. But his greatest trust was placed in Justin Ferrington, Lord Lonsdale.

Although the wars were over, there were loose ends to be tied together, and the English delegation led by Lord Castlereagh had continuing need of information, most usually gathered by stealth, about the other powers.

The Ferringtons, therefore, were at the moment relaxing in the exciting city of Vienna. During the war years, Francis Ferrington, now at the window of the salon watching wayward flakes of snow drift down, had grown up. Justin knew this, and of himself he thought, I've grown old. He longed only to live in peace, to see again his home in England, take long walks across his broad acres, hounds at his heels, and no gun in the crook of his arm. But he was in Vienna, still in the service of the English mission under Castlereagh, in whose palace he was now living.

This spacious room was well furnished in the French fashion, and Justin found his present surroundings pleasant indeed. He said as much to Francis.

"I find every room in Vienna excessively hot," Francis told him crossly.

"Rather be on bivouac?" Justin queried, a quizzical note in his voice.

Francis turned away from the window and laughed. He was a reasonably pleasant-featured man with no claims to handsomeness, but his frank and open expression lent him attractiveness. He appeared young and eager, but his deep blue Ferrington eyes held an expression older than his years, reflecting experiences of war and death.

He had followed his adored cousin Justin into some very tight spots in their forays to learn more about the French army's situation than the enemy wanted Wellington to know. But Francis had gone only because he worshiped Justin. He himself lacked that wicked, daredevil quality that Justin must have inherited from his Gallic mother's family. No Ferrington ever risked disaster—at least willingly.

Justin consulted his gold quarter repeater made for him by the London watchmaker Robert Pennington. Such a confoundedly early hour to pay a call, he thought, especially the particular call that lay just ahead of him.

He had been summoned by an old woman connected to him only by her marriage to a now deceased cousin of his father's. It was not a duty he looked forward to. "If I had suspected for one moment, Francis," he said in his deep, pleasant voice, "that Cousin Maria had uprooted herself and settled in Vienna, I should have found an errand in Paris, or perhaps Moscow."

Francis laughed. "I count my blessings, Justin. She sent for you, not me."

"May I remind you, cub, that you stand in the same kinship as I do to the duchess?"

"I am well aware of that misfortune. I may count on you not to remind her?"

Justin flashed a glance at him. "I should not take my good nature for granted, if I were you."

Francis laughed again, but this time amusement formed only one part of it. He had good reason to believe that Justin would never betray him. Justin had often enough in recent years been the rock to which Francis had trusted his life. More than one scrape might well have proved the end for Francis, had it not been for Justin's wit and, occasionally, marksmanship. The single time that it had been in Francis's power to extricate Justin from a tight place Francis brushed aside. It was the least he owed Justin, he pointed out, but the two men, eight years' difference in their ages, had as a result of their efforts for Wellington grown close as brothers.

"What do you think she wants of you, Justin?"

"Probably to terrify me," said Justin equably. "In my youth she adored seeing me tremble before her. I suspect I shall do so again."

"You, afraid of a frail old woman? After that gun duel in Valladolid?"

"You've lost the point, Francis. A gun fires once and either you're alive or you are not. But our dear Cousin Maria goes on and on. She is a devotee of a variant upon the water torture I believe the Chinese have perfected."

Francis turned thoughtful. "If you want me to accompany you, I will. But I warn you, if she has chosen a bride for you, I shall not be able to maintain my gravity."

"Bride?" Justin glared, outraged, at his cousin. "I should hope not! I can fix my interest for myself."

Francis was in a quizzing mood. "Sometimes I have thought your interest was already fixed."

"Not at all! I have not been in England for two years, remember."

Indeed Francis did. It was when Justin returned from that leave that he had seemed different, somehow abstracted. Francis had suspected that a female was on his cousin's mind, but he dared not probe, and Justin never vouchsafed any confidences.

Justin smiled, the sweet smile that could inspire such devotion that his men, or Francis, would follow him anywhere. "My thanks. But do you know, I feel that one bleeding Ferrington corpse is quite enough."

Cousin Maria, Duchesse de Carignac, had managed to install herself in a wing of the Kaunitz Palace, the quarters provided for Talleyrand and the rest of the French delegation.

Guided through huge rooms hung with Gobelin tapestries and furnished with elegant brocaded chairs—and each containing that ubiquitous fixture in every Viennese room, a porcelain stove throwing out immense amounts of heat for a short distance—at length he was met by a cross dragon named Hannah and shown into the presence of the duchess.

"There you are!" she cried.

"As you see," he said quietly, advancing to bow over her hand. "I trust I see you well."

"As well as these Frenchies let me be," she retorted. She was a large woman, stout to the point of near immobility. Her head was wrapped in an enormous turban, fastened with a brooch fashioned of cabochon sapphires surrounded by diamonds. Her fingers were stiff with rings, and the jewels in them flashed as she drew a rug over her knees.

She was seated on a small sofa—a chair would have been entirely inadequate to deal with her weight. Next to her a table had been placed, on which was displayed an assortment of excessively large, ill-cared-for jewelry.

Justin was far too polite to stare, but he was adept at looking from the corners of his eyes. Good God! The woman must carry her entire fortune with her on her wrists and around her neck. A closer look, however, turned him thoughtful on more than one head.

After the duchess had inquired as to the health of various Ferrington relatives, whose names he could hardly remember and of whose current status he was entirely ignorant, she paused and regarded him fixedly. As though assessing the worth of a prize bull, he thought with sudden amusement. How vulgar he had grown! A good thing he was presently staying in Vienna—for he was not fit for conversing in a London drawing room.

"You remember my brother Rupert." It was not a question, so he did not feel required to answer, but in truth her brother Rupert had entirely escaped his notice during his own lifetime. "Well, he's dead."

"I'm sorry."

"Don't be. He was a pigheaded old idiot, and nobody could make him see reason."

Justin correctly translated this to mean that she had lost their most recent argument. Even though Sir Rupert was a stranger to him, he knew Cousin Maria, and only one argument with her was an impossibility. There must have been a running series of disagreements.

"Insisted on jumping a quirky stallion," she elaborated. "Did for him. That's not the point."

"There is a point?" he murmured.

"He's left this daughter," the duchess said, ignoring his comment. "And I've got to have her."

"Why?"

"Duty. I'm her only kin. All I have will be hers."

"How fortunate for her!" Justin murmured.

"And I have a husband for her."

He glanced sharply at the duchess, but caught no answering gleam in her eye. He was overly sensitive, he decided, because of Francis's teasing.

"Is there not a Lady Morland?" he inquired after a moment.

Cousin Maria set herself, with a gusty sigh of resignation, to explaining the situation at Morland Hall. "So there's nobody but that interfering stepsister of hers to object. Do you know, she had the unmitigated brass to write—" The duchess broke off. Cunningly, she resumed, "The child may not wish to come. But with your address you can win Almira over."

A chill crept down Justin's spine. He suspected that he was about to be presented with an outrageous demand far outstripping whatever obligation Cousin Maria had saddled him with in the past. He braced himself to refuse point-blank and with dogged determination.

"Win her over?" His voice rasped.

"To come to Vienna. That's all I ask of you, Justin, and it's little enough."

Quite a half hour later, he was still refusing, but with diminishing vigor. Sensing victory, Cousin Maria pounced. "Then you'll do it, Justin. I truly do not see why you are making these idiotic objections to a simple errand."

"You expect me—let me see whether I understand you aright—you wish me to travel across the Continent in midwinter, find some obscure manor house in Kent called Morland Hall, and bring a schoolroom miss back with me?"

"So I have been saying for this long time, Justin. I had not thought you a lackwit."

"Nor I you, Cousin. But you must see how completely ineligible this scheme is. You cannot expect me to escort a wellbred young lady from London to Vienna."

"She'll be chaperoned, of course," said the duchess impatiently, "and certainly I can count on you to do the decent thing. I have no fear that she'll arrive compromised."

"If you expect me to be your errand boy, you need have no fear that she will arrive at all."

"Nonsense. I know there's no need to tempt you with money. You're indecently rich. But I wonder—" She broke off, her little eyes glancing slyly at her visitor. "I tell you what I shall do, Justin. I see that you are for some reason reluctant to do me the simplest favor. So in response to your delicate feelings, which you are trying to bam me into believing are real, I shall rescind my request."

"I am greatly relieved," he said formally. "I should not have agreed in any case, but it is much more comfortable not to have any cause to disagreement between us. Pray tell me, are you finding Vienna to your liking?"

"If that renegade bishop Talleyrand comes through, I'll like it better. Do you know he had the effrontery to tell me that I have no hope of getting back the Carignac estates?"

"Back, Cousin Maria? They were never yours."

"Of course they're mine. My dear Etienne left them to me. And just because some idiotic government gave the estates to one of their riffraff doesn't mean—"

"I do know something of this, Cousin. My own lands were sequestered, confiscated, whatever term they used."

"Of course, your mother was French," said Cousin Maria in a dismissing tone. "Got your lands back?"

Justin forbore to inform her that he had never truly lost them, that the tenants of his mother's family had been exceedingly loyal to their excellent masters, and that, in truth, much of his success in penetrating the schemes of Bonaparte's armies in Spain was due to information reaching him from his trusted people in Limousin.

Taking his silence for an answer, she snorted, "Thought not. Believe me, I'll get mine."

The rest of the visit passed in apparent amiability. When Justin rose to take his leave, she grinned at him. "Forgot to tell you. Remember my nephew Neil? From my second marriage."

Remembering without pleasure the last time he had seen Neil, in the hands of guards, awaiting court-martial for various sins, Justin admitted, "I remember him."

"Didn't like him, I see. Neither did I. But he was an interesting fellow, just the same. On his last leave, before the—the incident, he told me a few things about young Francis. That time he got away with a wagon train of grain for Wellington's men? And sold it for himself? I thought I'd die a-laughing."

Justin turned cold. He fixed his cousin by marriage with an icy stare. "That's not the way it was! It was Neil who stole from his starving men. That was why he was—shot." Even dead, Neil seemed to be a festering thorn.

Her grin widened. "I suppose not. Never heard of a Ferrington with sticky fingers. But just the same, it makes a good story, doesn't it? Might make a prospective bride think twice about young Francis, don't you agree?"

Justin felt his fingers clench into fists. He should have known that the old woman would not hesitate to stoop to blackmail. Not for the first time, he wondered how she had managed to snare his father's cousin, but of course she had been young and most likely more attractive than she appeared today. With an effort he managed not to reveal more than a hint of the strong dislike he felt for her.

"I see," he said with barely suppressed fury, "that you intend to force me to trot across Europe with your niece."

"I asked you nicely at the first," she said with revolting demureness.

Lord Lonsdale knew when he was defeated. He could face down any calumny on himself, but young Francis was not yet well known in society. A breath of scandal no matter how untrue could effectively blast his reputation and in all likelihood ruin his life.

"I suppose I must," said Justin, apparently calm. "I suspect that conceding to your wishes will be more enjoyable than staying in Vienna with the prospect of hearing a daily lecture from you on the subject."

He turned to go. This time he examined the mound of jewels with obvious deliberation. "Good God, Cousin," he exclaimed, "why aren't these put away safely? There's a tiara that I know belonged to my grandmother, and was not your Ferrington husband's to give you. That excessively vulgar ruby necklace? *That* I suppose you purchased for yourself."

"No need to be insulting," she said crisply. "The jewels are mine, and I like to look at them. That tiara, Justin, will come back to you only if a court decides, and—of course—if it can then be found."

"You know I shall not go to court over that bauble," he said at the door. "I have been neglectful recently, I fear, but from now on I shall thank God daily that I am kin to you only by marriage."

He shut the door quietly behind him, and allowed himself a deep breath. God, how near he had come to violence! The Bible recommended smiting hip and thigh, and although he had never raised his hand to a woman, he did not make himself any promises for the future.

He walked briskly along the Ringstrasse, letting the frigid autumn air cool his heated temper. In recent years, he believed, he had mastered the temper that was his inheritance. Certainly no one could have survived the past six years in the midst of the Peninsular Wars except by cool-headedness.

Was the threat that made him capitulate to the old witch a real one? He believed so, or he would not have given in. She would think nothing of ruining Francis's reputation in England, so that careful mothers kept their daughters away from a scoundrel who would steal from his own men. And since Francis had given up his years on the town, so to speak, to slog with Justin through Portugal and Spain, it was up to him to see that his cousin did not suffer unduly from the sacrifice.

An unpleasant thought occurred to him. Suppose Francis had gone with him to call on Cousin Maria, and she had threatened him to his face! Francis must never learn of the old lady's threats. Francis had not yet the rigid control of the Ferrington temper that Justin had learned.

And Justin himself had come so close to losing his own—he could almost feel that thick throat encompassed within his long thin fingers. But he was back in civilization now.

He smiled wryly to himself, and after an hour turned back toward his rooms.

CHAPTER 7

Now, half a continent away, Justin Ferrington looked down upon the slightly built girl he held in his arms, and below the surface of his mind an obscure memory stirred, and vanished before he could recognize it. The hood of her cloak had fallen back, and her light brown hair tumbled around her face, partly hiding her features. Could this be the hobbledehoy from Morland Hall, the niece of his nemesis Cousin Maria? He shuddered at the thought of traveling back to Vienna with a young miss so awkward that she could not step down from a stile.

Sitting on the ground, Corinna could feel the cold earth sending a chill creeping unpleasantly along her legs. This entire incident, the curious development by which she had entered a marvelous dream world, could not be real, and yet she could smell pungent tobacco and starchy fresh linen.

She shivered, and Lord Lonsdale relaxed his hold on her. "Are you injured?" His voice seemed unnecessarily cool, and it provoked a salutary state of mind in her.

She struggled to her feet, his powerful arm assisting her. As she bent down to straighten the folds of her cloak, her face was hidden from him, and he did not see the shock of recognition still in her eyes. Nor, to be fair, would he have understood it. Her regrets for the unseemly occurrence were confused and sadly lacking in coherence. But, apologies over, she regained her wits.

"I fear I must have seemed quite rude, sir." No use letting him know that she recognized his features—after all, they had never been introduced. "I must suppose you have business at Morland Hall, and in that case, you know, I shall hear of it eventually."

He appeared to be puzzled. Perhaps he had remembered that tiny moment of mutual interest, two years ago, and come to find her! She waited in hope for his answer. She was disappointed.

"Are you perhaps Miss Morland?"

So. He had come for Almira. "No, certainly I am not."

The bald statement took him aback. "Then—"

"You will not like to let your horses stand," she said crisply. "If you go on, you cannot miss the gates."

"I am persuaded," he said after a quick look into her face, where even in the fading light he could see her lips were blue with cold, "that you must not stay here. Is there no house nearby where I may take you? Were you on foot? I see no conveyance at hand."

She did not respond at once. He was in a dilemma. He must not leave even a female who appeared uncivil, even a gauche female, alone on a lonely road with night and possibly a storm coming on. "May I take you to Morland Hall? At least you will be more comfortable there."

"It is not at all necessary," she said, but her feet were stumps of cold and her lips were stiff. She was enormously relieved when the decision was taken out of her hands. She did not know quite how it happened, but she was handed up into the curricle, and the groom turned the reins over to Justin and sprang up behind for the short ride to Morland Hall.

If Justin spoke, to beguile the time, she did not know it. Her thoughts raced like mice fleeing a purposeful cat, around and around in confusion. What was he doing here? If he had not come to seek her out, having remembered her from that one moment in Almack's, then why? He thought she was Almira—therefore he did not know the girl. And obviously he did not remember Corinna.

Was he about to offer for a schoolroom miss whom he had never seen? Impossible—she hoped. But he had asked most specifically for Morland Hall.

Suddenly giddy with excitement, she wondered absurdly if he had come to carry off Emma Sanford. She was hard put to restrain a giggle.

If her own astonishment at meeting Lord Lonsdale on the road had been keen, still stronger was the impact of her arrival, supported up the steps by an elegant stranger, on the Morland servants.

Brixton, opening the door upon hearing the approaching vehicle on the gravel drive, allowed his jaw to drop while he stared at the smart rig, from which descended a tall man, garbed in a many-caped driving coat in the height of fashion. A groom had descended and gone sharply to the heads of the splendid pair of blacks blowing steam in the cold air. The gentleman turned to help his passenger to the ground.

A whisper escaped the butler's lips. "Miss Corinna!" Then he gestured fiercely to the footman crowding closely behind him in the doorway.

Corinna had put her thoughts to some purpose as they had come up the winding drive, and now as she ran up the steps to the entrance porch—her feet were coming uncomfortably back to life, and she winced—she spoke to Brixton. "Do not stand in the way, Brixton. Send for someone to show the groom the way to the stables, and see that he has refreshment. And please bring coffee to the drawing room."

She turned then, with an air of guilelessness, to her companion. "This is Brixton. But—I fear I do not know your name, sir?"

For a fleeting moment, as he saw Corinna in the full light of the foyer of Morland Hall, something stirred again in him, some recognition, some evocation of a past meeting. It could not be, of course, for she seemed very young, and he had not been in London for some time. But she was clearly of a quality other than that of his first impression of her. He told her his name.

Shortly, she led the way into the drawing room. "Now we can be comfortable," she said brightly, "and you may tell me your purpose at Morland Hall." She seated herself in a chair near the fire and looked up at him.

Justin, to his surprise, labored under a strange sense of dislocation. He had come scorching alone accompanied only by his groom, Grimsby, across Europe, driven by anger at his Cousin Maria's bald threat to ruin Francis, to find some schoolgirl in the wilds of Kent and take her to Vienna. He would never have entertained even the possibility that the mission might be anything other than dreadful. He had hoped only that he could dispatch his business quickly, turn the child over to the untender mercies of the duchess, gather up Francis in Vienna, and vanish.

Francis, a devoted and faithful companion during the dangerous years, was at an age where settling down to country life on his substantial estates seemed desirable. As a Ferrington, he could expect to marry well—if Cousin Maria's vicious tongue could be stilled. Unfortunately, Justin had mused, there was only one civilized way to deal with her, and at this moment he was launched on this endeavor.

But if this young lady before him, with the appealing hazel eyes and the generous mouth, was not Miss Morland, then who in the devil was she?

With studied remoteness, he said, "My business, I fear, is with Miss Morland. I have a letter for her attention. May I be announced to her?"

"Isn't it more usual to—?" Her voice died away. She had guessed that Lord Lonsdale had come to make an offer to Almira. There was absolutely no other reason for his visit—none in the world.

"To—?" His deep pleasant voice held a question.

"Should you not approach her through her trustees?"

"What do they have to do with anything?" Justin was losing his grip on his temper. This baffling slip of a girl with the enormous eyes was deliberately putting obstacles in his way, and he did not even know who she was. He glared at her, only to discover a laugh in her eyes. Suddenly his ill temper fled, and he smiled.

"I fear we are dealing at cross purposes," he said, "and while I do not know who you are, yet I suspect I shall do better if I take you into my confidence."

"Pray do."

He explained his errand. Pruned of the duchess's outrageous threats, and of his consequent ill temper, the tale was soon told.

"And you have come all the way from Vienna," Corinna marveled, "simply to take Almira to her aunt?"

He nodded. "Put like that, I am not surprised at your reluctance to believe me. Miss—?"

"I am Corinna Darley," she told him, and explained her situation at Morland Hall. "Yes, I do believe you. It is the duchess whose expectations astonish me. When I wrote to her explaining my stepsister's situation, I expected a reply from London, or perhaps Paris at the farthest. At best, I hoped for a leisurely winter, preparing for Almira's Season under the sponsorship of the duchess." She reflected a moment. "I do not scruple to tell you, Lord Lonsdale, that I have never understood Almira's aunt."

"No more do I."

"But then you are not related to her either?"

"I thank God I am not."

Suddenly she chuckled, a sound that appealed enormously to him. "I hesitate to believe that she considers my stepsister such an addlepate as to rush into foreign lands with a stranger as escort! I cannot think so. The duchess cannot be so lost to propriety."

Justin agreed. "She did mention a chaperon. Could she have meant you, do you think?"

"No, I am sure not. Emma Sanford resides with us, in the capacity of Almira's governess, chaperon, companion. I should insist upon her accompanying Almira, you know."

"I should not dream of any lesser arrangement," he agreed heartily.

"Well, then," said Corinna practically, "we may as well see at once what Almira wishes to do."

Good God, thought Justin, does she have a choice? Her aunt had sent for her, and therefore, in Justin's mind, the issue was not to be questioned. Any well-brought-up young lady would quite simply have wept with excitement at the prospect of foreign travel, made a thousand objections that she had need of trunks full of new clothes, and at once set to packing with a will. Had he been away from England for too long?

He did not realize that he had spoken aloud until his eyes met the level gaze of Miss Darley's clear hazel eyes. He could not be sure, but he fancied he caught a glimpse of amusement lurking in the gray depths.

"My stepsister, you must know, is very young." He detected an undercurrent of significance, but at the moment he could not identify it. His worst imaginings dealt swiftly with the idea that the girl might be at the least an antidote, or even, save the mark, a defective.

Corinna saw with approval that Lord Lonsdale's expression smoothed out as though ironed, and all trace of indignation was quite properly stifled. A man one could count on, she thought—a man thoroughly in control of himself.

When Miss Sanford shepherded Almira into the room, Justin stood for a long moment as though rooted to the floor. Corinna performed introductions, and when they were all seated, she said with a bland expression, "Lord Lonsdale has something of import to say to you."

He threw Corinna a glance full of appeal. Had she intentionally framed her speech to make it sound as though he were about to offer for the child?

Perhaps hearing how the words sounded had caught Corinna's ear as well. At least, she continued, "He has come from your aunt, Almira. The duchess wishes you to join her. In Vienna."

"Vienna?" The word was merely formed on Almira's lips, without breath. Justin took note of the perfection of her heart-shaped face and the enticing dark ringlets that were prone to bounce delightfully when she turned her head, as she did now.

"Lord Lonsdale, I cannot—oh, dear, I do not know quite—what a coil! I do not know what Ja—" She broke off.

"Almira, my dear." Miss Sanford sounded a warning note.

However, Almira paid her no heed, instead putting her hands up to cover her face. A strangled sound as of a sob escaped through her fingers.

Throwing Justin a hasty glance, Corinna crossed to kneel beside her stepsister. "Almira, pray recollect your manners!" she said in a most coaxing voice. "I confess I am astonished at your behavior. What do you mean, you cannot? Is not this what you have been wishing for this long time? To be presented to society?" It occurred to Corinna that the duchess had not made such a precise offer. But no matter. Almira had taught her family to grasp hurriedly at short-term solutions.

Justin, acutely embarrassed, could think of no route of escape. He had been many times in peril of his life, among an alien people and in enemy hands, and always his brain had worked at fever pitch to extricate him from predicament.

Now, he was stunned at the strong wish that visited him, as alien as any wish had ever been. Simply put, he wished to take that vexatious child by the shoulders and shake some sense into her, and leave the purlieus of Morland Hall within the hour. And—unbelievably—he wished to rescue Miss Darley and take her with him.

By the time he had shaken off such an aberration, and returned in his mind to the company in the salon, he was much relieved to see that Miss Morland was smiling tremulously, her dark lashes wet upon her cheeks, and addressing him.

"Pray forgive me, Lord Lonsdale," she said prettily, "but I was so shocked by your news. I had thought my aunt had quite forgotten me."

She had written to her, she had told Corinna. Now Corinna, substantially surprised at the duchess's response to Almira, even though she had not deigned to write to Corinna, realized that at the first she had not believed Almira.

Now she knew she had heard truth. But Almira had asked for dowry money. It was abundantly clear, Corinna realized, looking out of the corner of her eyes at the elegant visitor, that while the duchess might take an interest in her niece, such concern would be expressed under her own supervision.

Almira was clearly prepared, now that she had begun to explain, to continue on explaining the rift between her papa and the duchess. Knowing Almira's prolix tendencies, Corinna sent a meaningful glance at Emma Sanford and turned to Lord Lonsdale.

"I believe we shall be better able on the morrow to consider what is best to be done," she said, practically. "Certainly Almira must consider the duchess's wishes, but you see, we are still in mourning for Sir Rupert, and I am not precisely sure what Mr. Treffingham—Almira's trustee, you know—will wish her to do . . ."

Her voice trailed off. She was sure a long evening lay ahead, coaxing Almira into a better humor, going over with Almira, and then Emma, and more than likely again with Almira, the letter to Almira from the duchess, brought by Justin, which lay unopened upon the little table next to her chair.

Miss Sanford interrupted. "I believe Almira will wish to wash her face," she said with resolution, clutching her charge firmly by the wrist, "and I beg you to excuse us, Lord Lonsdale."

When Justin was left alone with Corinna, he looked at her for some moments with sympathy. At length, the silence becoming noticeable to her, she looked up to find, to her great surprise, a gleam of understanding in his expression.

"How long," he said gently, "have you been in charge—here at Morland Hall?"

"Nearly a year," she answered. "My stepfather died of a fall from a horse, and there was no time for him to arrange properly for his daughter. Of course, since my mother died two years ago, I have managed the establishment for Sir Rupert. You must know that I am most grateful to him, for he kept me here after my mother died, and he was not obliged to do so."

"Well," he said, "I do not wish to outstay my welcome. I have lodgings in Wrotham for the night. If you do not object, may I call upon you tomorrow to see what news I may send to the duchess?"

"Of course you may," she said simply, rising and placing her hand in his outstretched one. "Perhaps you will remain to join us for dinner this afternoon?"

"I think not. I do not like to drive on roads I do not know well in such cloudy darkness. I shall hope to arrive at Wrotham before rain sets in."

His rare smile accompanied his refusal, and she felt again as she had that one moment when their eyes had met across a room thronged with people. Clearly, she thought ruefully after he had left, even after being in company for an hour or two, that precious instant had not recalled itself to his memory.

Or, if it had, it had meant nothing to him. Surely his dreams had not included her! And rightly so, she told herself firmly. Only chance had brought him into her life at this moment, and chance could, and likely would, remove him as quickly.

Picking up the letter from the duchess, addressed

in a crabbed hand to Miss Almira Morland, Corinna looked at it without seeing it.

Now that she had leisure to consider, she realized that Almira's response to the magnificent prospect of traveling to Vienna was odd, at the least. Imagine, after a short time of exciting and educational travel, arriving at the capital of Austria, crowded at this moment with the aristocracy of four countries, in a glittering assembly of diplomats working out peace after the confinement of Napoleon on the island of Elba, in the company—no small consideration, this—of Lord Lonsdale.

And Almira said she couldn't?

Setting her lips firmly, Corinna left the room, crossed the entrance hall, and started up the stairs.

Almira could—Corinna promised herself—and she would!

CHAPTER 8

The Morland traveling coach, refurbished in great haste and made ready for the road, was nearing Dover, and for the first time in some days, Corinna had time to think about the extraordinary events that had taken place.

The days intervening between Justin Ferrington's visit conveying Aunt Maria's message and the departure of the party from Morland Hall had been filled with scurrying dressmakers, fits of hysteria on the part of Almira's maid, Nellie, who looked forward to the certain fate of being murdered in her bed by unsavory foreigners smelling of garlic, increasingly deep furrows of worry on the brow of Emma Sanford, and a constant stream of visitors apparently to wish them well on their journey, but more intent on wringing from Corinna the last detail of such an odd expedition.

Corinna was too fully engaged in preparations to pay great heed to Almira's moods. In truth, they swung so widely that it would have been difficult to follow them, although one factor remained constant: Almira toiled not, neither did she spin. Instead, she entertained Corinna and Emma with a constantly changing kaleidoscope of emotional crises.

One day she would be ecstatically looking forward to great society in Vienna, the next she was abstracted, unheeding when spoken to, and, if strongly encouraged, seemed to emerge from some trancelike state. Whatever arguments were presented to her on the desirability of acceding with high heart and cheerful mien to her aunt's disposition of her immediate future were lost, because she refused to listen.

One day, as preparations for the journey threatened to tie themselves into a Gordian knot, capable of being loosened by drastic measures only, such as a ruinous fire, Emma encountered Corinna in the upper hall. Emma was struggling with armfuls of what appeared to be undergarments. "Could you open that door for me, please? These silks slide like eels, and I am afraid I shall drop them."

Corinna obliged, and followed her into the upstairs sitting room. At one time, when Corinna and her mother first came to Morland Hall, this room had been refurnished as a sitting room for the new Lady Morland. It was painted in creams and deep rose, with deft touches of apple green—colors which complemented to great effect the rich auburn hair and dark gray eyes of Corinna's mother.

Now, however, the room was in great disarray. Trunks stood open everywhere, gowns and slippers and shawls spilling out, other clothing in piles ready to pack. On several tables were clustered jars of creams and soaps, phials of remedies against the headache and motion sickness, and laudanum and oil of cloves in case of the toothache.

Emma deposited her burden and swept two chairs clear of their burdens.

"I want to talk to you," she said soberly. "About Almira."

Corinna's heart sank. "What has she done now? Decided once again she is not going to Vienna?"

"No. I think between us we have convinced her that she has no choice. After all, if she refuses the help of her only relative, what more is there? No, it seems to me she is spending far too much time with young Jack Hardie."

Corinna was surprised. "But I have not seen him . . ." Her voice trailed off. "Now that you mention it, I recall that she has been absent a good deal. Mostly when I needed to talk to her about something."

"Ah, yes, you see it too."

"But I did not know she was with Jack." After a moment, she confessed, "I really have not paid attention to her at all. I can understand her reluctance to leave him." Her heart sank. "You don't think she really does not intend to go to Vienna? After all *this*?" Corinna gestured at the untidy result of two weeks of intense planning.

"But she knows that the dowry business was nonsense!"

"I fear your good heart has betrayed you into ignoring any ominous signs. My experience, in more than one household, you know, tells me that Almira gives every indication of strong attachment."

"Well, of course she is sorry to leave him. They were talking about marriage, after all."

Emma spoke doubtfully. "Were they?"

Corinna stared. "Dowry was mentioned, I believe. And that surely indicates marriage?"

"Dowry," Emma pointed out in a practical manner, "simply means money."

"To be handed over upon marriage."

"Or betrothal, as I have occasionally seen."

"They could not expect to be betrothed for at least two years. Emma, you know something you have not told me!"

Emma tiptoed to the door to make sure it was safely closed. "Sit down, Corinna. This may take some time. . . ."

*   *   *

Now, in the coach rumbling on its way to Dover, she went over in her mind the news that Emma had relayed to her that day. Corinna could not but feel relief that they were well out of Kent. Jack had become a threat that she would not have known how to deal with.

Emma's whispered voice still spoke in her memory. "Jack has become quite a figure in Wrotham," she had said. "He has made some friends among the lower classes—he is deeply in debt to gamblers who are not particular how they recover their winnings—"

"Do you mean," Corinna had demanded, shocked, "that he wanted Almira's dowry for himself, to pay off his debts? Surely he could not have expected any sum of money in his hands for months and months!"

"You can be sure Mr. Treffingham would take good care of Almira's interests. That is why, I surmise, Jack wished Almira to ask for money from the duchess. Mr. Treffingham would know nothing of that, and Jack would be bound to no agreements."

"How dastardly!"

Eventually, Corinna rose. She embraced Emma fondly. "You are such a good friend. I beg you not to worry. We will keep her close until we leave. When we are actually on the road to Vienna, she is sure to forget him. She will be meeting many new people. Remember, much of Jack's appeal must be that he is the only young friend she has here. And while he is older, and his reputation indicates that he is more experienced, I have no doubt that when we start, we will have seen the last of Jack Hardie."

The conversation with Emma was not the only unsettling occurrence of that day. Early in the afternoon, Lord Lonsdale was announced to Corinna.

Quickly she smoothed down her hair, bit her lips to make them redder, and hurried downstairs to the drawing room.

"I am so pleased to see you," she told him, thinking again how odd it was to have the man who had crept into her dreams, infrequently but without rivalry, turn into a three-dimensional gentleman coming toward her across the room.

"You appear to be in good spirits," he said, but his eyes were questioning.

"Should I not be? Mr. Treffingham has decreed that I go with Almira to Vienna, since he feels Emma is not sufficiently capable. Fustian! She is more competent than I by far." She was gratified to note an answering glint in his eyes—a response she hoped was pleasure at the prospect of her company on the journey. A doubt assailed her. "Is it possible that you wish to leave earlier than planned? I confess we are not ready to rope all the trunks to the coach and set off down the drive. For one thing, Mr. Treffingham's guards are not to arrive for another sennight."

"Guards?" asked Justin, at a loss.

"Almira's trustee, you know. He insisted that we travel like royalty with armed guards before us and behind us. I should not think they are required. Even though I cannot alter Mr. Treffingham's arrangements, I should like your opinion."

"Armed guards. Well, I have been out of England for some years and perhaps am out of tune with the times."

An odd note in his voice alarmed her. "You do think we need protection of that sort!"

"Miss Darley, I would never have thought that traveling with a platoon of armed men was necessary in England. But on the way here, from Wrotham, I was forced to change my mind."

Then she looked at him with care. "Your cheek!"

He raised his hand to touch the place on his cheekbone that was beginning to throb, and his fingers came away bloody. At once he was taken in charge, and his wound cleaned.

"A bullet, Lord Lonsdale?"

The bullet had come from ambush, he told her while she dressed his wound with fingers that at times shook, and he had not seen anyone. "Merely grazed, I am certain. No doubt a stray shot by a hunter," he said casually, but he had recognized the sound of the shot, and it had not come from a hunting gun.

Perhaps the wound had already made him feverish. There was no other reason, thought Miss Darley in rosy speculation, for him to hold the hand that smoothed salve on his wound and say, "Could you not call me Justin—Corinna?"

And now they were indeed on the road, and their destination for the day loomed ahead of them. Dover Castle, huge and bulky on the skyline, led them for an hour as they neared. There was time to remember all the history that wrapped itself into Dover—the armies leaving for Calais, which was then English territory; Henry the Eighth with his enormous royal retinue bound for the famous meeting with the French king on the Field of the Cloth of Gold; Charles the Second returning to his homeland, to the enormous relief of his subjects.

Emma, less romantically inclined, said, "I hope the beds are well aired. It will not do for Almira to take cold."

"Nor any of us," Corinna added, just avoiding a touch of dryness in her words.

"But a cold is more dangerous when one is out of temper."

The party clopped into Dover and drew up before the Ship. It was quite a procession, led by the great traveling chariot, bearing Emma, Corinna, and Almira on their way to unknown parts.

Lord Lonsdale traveled behind them in his smart curricle, with Almira's servants following in a coach with the luggage. When they crossed the Channel, all the servants except Nellie would be left behind. The outriders hired by Mr. Treffingham were armed and numerous.

Mr. Treffingham's sudden generosity in the matter of Almira's journey could be laid to the prospect of getting Miss Morland out of the country for a bit. He had heard something of the girl's vagaries from Corinna, with whom he was on excellent terms. He did not even balk at the charges sure to be incurred for clothing and other incidentals to be acquired in Vienna. His hidden elation was entirely at the thought that the duchess, and not he, would be in charge of this young marriageable miss.

Mr. Treffingham, privately with Corinna, asked very kindly, "Shall you return from Vienna when you have delivered Miss Morland to her aunt?"

"I had not thought so far ahead," confessed Corinna. "It might be pleasant to stay on and see the great capital. So many notables there, you know, and there will never again be such an assemblage."

"No doubt, no doubt."

Also, and this she did not mention to Mr. Treffingham, she entertained a hope that Lord Lonsdale, having escorted them from England, would remain for a time in Vienna. She told herself she had long since given up hope of a serious entanglement, with Justin or anyone else, but she did think it was delightful to be in the company of a man of experience and knowledge.

He had not lingered in the vicinity of Morland

Hall after he had obtained Almira's consent to the expedition. Claiming affairs needing attention on his own estates, he had come down to Morland Hall for an occasional day's visit, apparently to answer questions that might have arisen in the interim, or proffer advice on the many knotty problems that afflicted novice travelers.

And how comforting it was, thought Corinna, to have all the details of the journey taken out of her hands. Only in the company of Justin did she realize how heavy the burden had been—of running the household, of thinking how best to get Almira into the sphere of society where she belonged, and all without the means to accomplish it.

Now Dover was at hand. A night at the Ship, or more, depending on the weather. Perhaps they might have to linger for a week or even longer before the weather cleared sufficiently for the crossing. It was a journey of half a day in the best of times with the best of following winds, but sometimes it took two or three days.

No matter, thought Corinna, her heart curiously light. The prospect of several days in Justin's company did nothing to cast her down. But she must make sure that Almira was on her best behavior. She thought that Justin might not suffer fools gladly.

The Ship was one of the two respectable inns in this port city, and deserved its impeccable reputation. The dinner provided was excellent, even considering the travel-whetted appetite that Corinna brought to the table, set in a private sitting room. Justin did not join them.

"I have discovered that my young cousin Francis is here in Dover, at the King's Head," he explained to Corinna. "I must join him, and this evening speak to the captain of our packet boat. Perhaps he can predict how soon the weather will favor our crossing."

After dinner Almira, pleading headache, went upstairs, Nellie trailing, to bed.

Lingering over a cup of strong coffee, Corinna and Emma were for the first time in some days private. Always there had been the prospect of Almira bursting in, or, worse, servants lingering outside a closed door. Now they were two, and the inn servants did not count.

Corinna imperceptibly began to relax. The worst part of the journey was over, she thought—the decision to travel, the endless packing, the myriad of questions and doubts that had assailed her in the weeks it had taken to get them on the road.

But now the die was cast. They could not turn back. And while Corinna suspected that there might be physical discomforts ahead, at the least, the only way to go was forward. The decision having been made, she could give herself up to the pleasure of the journey and the prospect that lay ahead. As though to echo her own thoughts, Emma said slowly, "I wonder what her grace wants of Almira."

"She wants her company," said Corinna, a trifle sharply. "What else could she want? Almira is far from wealthy."

"And of course her grace has done well out of her English marriages. Her marriage to the duke—well, who knows? And it is none of my business anyway. But I should be greatly surprised if all she wants of Almira is her company."

Corinna was warned by a subtle note in Emma's voice. She regarded her friend soberly. "I think, Emma, you had better tell me precisely what is in your mind."

For a moment, Emma seemed not to heed her. Emma had had some experience with the species of nobility that could prove unreasonable and unpredictable. She had developed a deep distrust of persons in a superior class of society, for there was no one who could call them to account for misdeeds. Now she said to Corinna, "I wonder what her grace wants Almira to do."

Emma's doubts were always worth probing. "I do not understand what you mean."

"It may not be proper for me to say, but Almira's aunt never did anything without expecting a return. I have known her for some time, you know, since I came to Morland Hall while the first Lady Morland lived."

To Corinna's surprise, Emma's suspicions roused an echoing response in her own mind. "I do not know the lady well. I did not see much of her when she came two years ago, when she and Sir Rupert disagreed so strongly. I wonder whether we shall regret this decision."

Since there was no possible answer at this time, the subject was dropped. But Corinna began to speculate why Justin, who was after all in no way a dependent of anyone's, had done the duchess's bidding, accomplishing an errand she was sure he had not wished to execute. She knew that the duchess was, by marriage, a cousin of Justin's father, for he had told her so. But he had given no clue as to why he was serving as errand boy.

There was too much to think about. Corinna always thought better in the open air, and tonight especially she needed to be alone, in the freshness of the night.

The coffee would keep her awake, most likely, but if she walked for a bit, perhaps she could sleep.

She could not possibly sleep, besides, with a busy seaport just outside the window, a teeming and unknown city. She had devoured, in Sir Rupert's library, travel books by many explorers, all the way from Richard Hakluyt to Captain Cook, and at last she had an opportunity to explore, on a modest scale, of course, but entirely on her own, a town full of unexpected sights.

Picking up a cloak tossed casually over a chair in the sitting room, she donned it. Fastening the strings, she realized it was Almira's old one, suitable for traveling.

Corinna crossed to the door and slipped through into the black, windy night.

CHAPTER 9

Outside the inn, Corinna stopped, blinded by the darkness after the light inside. She breathed in the purely exotic scent of faraway places, of excitement, of adventure, of new sights and new people.

If someone had asked her only a month before what she would be doing on this very night, she could have told them with every confidence in her accuracy. She and Emma might be playing at piquet, whiling the time away before the bedtime tea cart. If she or Emma had gone that day into the village, there would be gentle narration of the trivia of rural life.

Even if someone had told her that in a month she would be standing on the doorstep of the Ship at Dover, making out the shadowy shapes of great sailing vessels just across the wide strip of pavement that edged the waterfront, she would promptly have marked him down as ready for Bedlam.

She closed her eyes, the better to detect the various scents that reached her nose. There was the sharp tang of what she thought must be oakum, and the noxious smell of what was generally called bilge, a smell that clutched unpleasantly at the throat. And a sour trace of malt, coming from the taverns, most likely, where the sailors refreshed themselves before the crossing. And after a crossing, also, she had no doubt.

From somewhere came the bitter smell of stale, overcooked coffee, and the unmistakable pungency of horses.

She opened her eyes. How surprising it was that the night was no longer as dark as the pitch that sealed the timbers of the vessels! There were stars overhead, showing the weather as fair. There was the far-off sound of voices, rising gustily as a tavern door opened, cut off sharply when it closed.

There was the stableyard wall, just to her left, bordering the street, and close at hand on her right a kind of half wall to provide shelter to those coming in or out of the inn. She would walk along the street parallel to the long wall, slowly, and then return to the safety of the inn.

She smiled, in the dark. Why would the word "safety" occur to her?

She glanced up at the prows of the ships tethered on short cables to the wharf. Somehow they seemed more massive than they had when she arrived that afternoon, looming larger than life, and in a way ominous.

Nonsense! she told herself, and stepped briskly to the pavement.

In the dark, her footing was uncertain, and she stepped with caution. Perhaps it had been foolish to leave the warm, well-lit comfort of the Ship's private parlor for this solitary stroll along the waterfront, but even while she doubted her good sense, she reveled in the gusts of wind that swooped around her.

There were craft as far as she could see, lying in the inner basin. She knew their names, but only in books. She could not have identified a brigantine, nor a hoy, nor even a Revenue cutter if her life depended on it. Which would be the packet on which their carriage would be loaded, their horses led below decks? On which of these boats, heaving gently in the harbor swell, would she leave England for the first time in her life? She hoped fervently it would be one of the larger vessels!

She had left behind, in the stuffy parlor, Emma and her doubts about the journey, and Almira's queer sullenness. The girl had written to her aunt requesting a dowry, and instead received a magnificent journey and the prospect of a giddy social whirl in Vienna. When she was Almira's age, Corinna would have seriously considered selling her soul for such a prospect.

Now, her soul was content with the prospect of a leisurely journey across Europe in the company of the most amusing, most cultured gentleman she knew. She suffered a small pang then, for she suspected guiltily that Justin would not approve of her lonely walk. But Justin had reserved rooms at the King's Head for himself and his cousin Francis, who was coming from Vienna to meet him at Dover.

Just then the wind died for a moment, and in the sudden silence she heard a scraping sound, as of boot on cobblestone. She stopped short and whirled to look behind her, straining her eyes to peer into the deep shadows. Nothing moved. A cat, probably, but she was not convinced. There was no time to think. From behind her an arm snaked out to encircle her waist, and she was swiveled sharply to face a stocky man, his breath sour with ale. The arm around her waist tightened and clutched her hard against his chest. One hand fumbled with her bonnet strings.

She cried out sharply in protest. In her ear came the rough words, "It's only me, love. Didn't I tell you I'd come?"

"You fool!" she cried out. "Let me go!"

Words alone would not save her. She twisted,

breaking his hold at first, but he seized her again, roughly. She kicked out, but she was wearing only soft leather slippers, and her kicks landed softly and without effect.

She writhed away from his foul breath, feeling her cloak slide from her shoulders as her assailant grasped her fiercely.

"Little love," he panted, "don't fight me. What's the matter?"

"Matter?" she cried out, her voice rising on the wind. "Let me go!" At last Corinna found her voice and emitted a loud, rousing cry.

With a growled curse, he released one hand and clapped it over her mouth. "Shut up, you idiot! I won't hurt you!"

Her scream had been heard. From ahead came the sound of running feet, hard on the cobbles, and warning shouts. Behind her the door to the Ship opened, and light streamed out into the street.

Now, aided by the stream of light, her assailant, through what she thought was his malt-fuddled brain, must have realized he had made a mistake. "Good God!" he muttered, in panic. He still held her by one hand, the other raised quickly to cover his own features. He shoved her violently away from him, and leaped over the wall.

Corinna could not keep her balance. She staggered a few steps, until her foot caught in the folds of Almira's cloak, dragging on the ground, and she fell, heavily.

The cobbles, uneven and lumpy beneath her body, felt wonderfully safe and comforting. She could willingly remain there, unstirring, for a day or two, probably becoming aware of soreness here, a bruise there. Most of all, she dreaded to move. Something might be broken and she might have to stay in

Dover! Vienna seemed to recede into a vague and blurred future.

But she was not to be allowed to rest, even on the cobbles. The footsteps she had heard approaching, the same footsteps that had frightened away her assailant, now came swiftly to her.

"Go after him, Francis! Over that wall! Watch out lest he double back!"

One set of footsteps receded into the distance, but the other remained. Corinna lay unmoving on the pavement.

Justin knelt beside her, touched her shoulder, and said, on a note that no one had heard in his voice for ten years or more, "Corinna!"

She was dead, he knew it, and a cold mass moved within his chest. He thrust back the cloak that lay half beneath her in a tangle, and, in the light streaming from the inn, he lifted her in his arms.

By this time the inn was alive with people rushing to the door. Francis returned to stand by him, sensing the distress in his cousin.

"He got over the wall and out of sight. Shall I take her?"

"Get this damned cloak away, if you can. I'll get her inside." Corinna, reluctant to return entirely to a world where people hit people and knocked them down, refused to open her eyes. She recognized as though from a distance that Justin held her, and even suspected—but she must be addled in her wits from the fall!—that he was more than ordinarily concerned.

She was not sure what had happened to her, save the assault itself, but Justin was holding her, and she was mightily comforted.

Carried into the inn, she was placed gently on a couch, and Almira's cloak was laid over her.

"She's cold!"

"But she wasn't gone long enough to get chilled. What happened?"

"Some villain attacked her!"

"Host, fetch a physician!"

In protest at this last, Corinna groaned. "No, pray do not. I am quite all right."

Emma said practically, "Of course you are, my dear, except for a great ugly bruise on your forehead, and your gown is torn."

"Oh dear, is it?" Corinna struggled to sit up, but since the world began to swing wildly around her, she thought it better to close her eyes and lay her head back.

"What's a torn gown, after all?" soothed Emma. "I will mend it myself tonight."

Justin had regained his composure. He was aware of his cousin Francis's bright eyes resting speculatively on him, but he refused to look up.

Almira joined them then, fully dressed. "What happened?" she demanded. "Oh, Corinna, were you foolish enough to go outside?"

Someone drew in an audible breath. Later Corinna thought that it was the natural result of Francis catching sight of the spectacularly beautiful Miss Morland for the first time.

"Tell us who attacked you," said Justin. "I will have the watch alerted. He cannot get far in the dark. What did he look like?"

"I cannot tell you who it was," said Corinna. "It was dark, and I could not see his face."

Someone nearby fetched a sigh almost of relief, but Corinna did not recognize the source. "But I do not think he meant to hurt me. I think he mistook me for someone else."

"What makes you think that?" Suddenly it was Justin Ferrington, advance intelligence man for the

Iron Duke, questioning a captive soldier. "What did he say?"

Corinna, quite naturally, resented the brisk impersonal questioning. "He said nothing," she said untruthfully, and added, "Nor did I ask him his name. Truly, Lord Lonsdale, there was neither time nor inclination to indulge in the amenities of conversation."

His eyes were hard and bright in sudden anger. Full of wrath, the expected reaction after such a fright as she had given him, he stood back from the couch. With a bite in his voice, he said, "You could have known this would happen."

"That I should be attacked?" she protested sharply.

"Any woman walking alone at night . . ." He let the sentence die away.

"I wasn't walking—at least, not yet."

He looked suspiciously at her. He suspected correctly that she had not been quite truthful with him. Was she hiding something? The corollary to that thought was an unpleasant one to take to bed with him.

After some bustle, Corinna too went to bed. She did not expect to sleep, for Nellie was a notorious snorer. She did not sleep for a short time. Her thoughts ran over the episode, until finally she realized that there was something in the back of her mind that eluded her. Just out of sight, the shadow of doubt loomed. Was there some detail about her attacker that she could bring to mind, something that would tell her—what?

It was impossible that she should know him. She had never been in Dover in her life.

If Corinna was hoping for a day of rest, she knew she would be disappointed when she opened her eyes the next morning. Sun was slipping through the slats of the shuttered window, and the day promised to be fine.

At breakfast, she found Emma already drinking her chocolate. "My dear girl," Emma exclaimed, "how do you feel after that terrible attack?"

"Truly, not as bad as I had expected," said Corinna, sliding into her seat and asking the waiter to bring her some hot coffee at once. "I fear I made a fool of myself last night, behaving as hen-witted as though something dreadful had happened to me."

"Certainly something did," said Emma with spirit. "Lord Lonsdale, I am persuaded, thought you were— past help."

"Lord Lonsdale grew quite impertinent," Corinna pointed out. "Does he think that I would not have told him who the man was, had I known?"

"Well," said Emma with an apologetic air, "perhaps he does. Indeed, Corinna dear, I confess to wondering myself whether there were not one or two things that perhaps had slipped your mind, in the circumstances."

"You too?" Corinna shot an accusing glance at her. "Well, I can see there is no use trying to deceive you. There was something. But I can't for the life of me tell you what it was. Something that niggles at the back of my mind."

"Then why did you not say so? Lord Lonsdale was much concerned."

"He went about his questioning in a far from delicate manner," said Corinna. "But there's no use talking about it. I can't remember. In fact, I was awake most of the night trying to think of what it might be."

"I am sure," said Emma, squinting good-naturedly, "that Nellie's snores aided you in concentrating."

Corinna laughed, and changed the subject. It

would make no difference how long she tried to remember—nothing would come to her. Perhaps the elusive scrap of information, or impression, would come to her sometime, possibly in the most unexpected circumstance. She would simply have to wait.

In the meantime, she turned her attention to Emma's gentle conversation.

"We are so fortunate that we will not have to wait in Dover. Do you know that a week of waiting is not in the least unusual? Only last century, dear Dr. Burney spent nine days here waiting for good weather."

"Of course, this is not a town in which to be immured," murmured Corinna. "Especially if one cannot set foot outside the inn. But surely the Ship could not take care of everyone who was forced to wait for fair weather?"

"Did you not notice as we came into Dover all the inn signs on the side streets? I should not like to stay at any one of them, since I should not trust the sheets to be aired properly."

Corinna looked from the window of their private sitting room, arranged for by Lord Lonsdale. She could see across the stableyard through the wide entrance to the sea beyond. The puffy white clouds were scampering across the sky, indicating a strong and favorable wind blowing toward Calais.

"With such a wind," remarked Emma, "we might be in Calais in half a day."

CHAPTER 10

The packet moved out of the inner basin into the outer harbor. Corinna felt the deck lift beneath her feet as the vessel met the chop in the Channel. While the swell in the harbor had been comparatively calm even under the stiff offshore breeze, the deep water lent itself to a longer fetch, and the motion required a different kind of balance.

"Come to the rail, Almira," suggested Corinna, noticing her stepsister's sudden pallor. "The wind is fresher here."

"If there is one thing I do not need," said Almira with spirit, "it is wind in my—" she gulped hastily—"face."

She turned precipitately and grabbed Emma's arm. "Help me. Where is our cabin?"

Mal de mer hit with the speed of lightning, thought Corinna. Almira was well one moment, and a pallid green color the next. There had been no moment between one breath—rather, one frenzied gulp of air—and the next to seek out the phial of laudanum packed for just such an emergency.

Since Nellie was below in the cabin, arranging some of the luggage, and Emma was already helping her to her bunk, Almira was in good hands. Corinna need not worry about her.

Setting off on her first real odyssey, Corinna felt her spirits rising in tune with the sea around her.

She touched her fingers to the swelling on her forehead. Exotic places—like Dover!—might have hidden dangers, like the worm at the heart of an apple.

She held to the rail with both hands. The wind blew strong from the shore, and already the mount of Dover Castle was dwindling in the distance. At this rate they might well make a record fast crossing. Corinna gave herself up to present enjoyment. The waves were the color of a slate roof, streaked with white and capped with foam.

Behind her lay Morland Hall with its uneventful life and provincial neighbors. She had longed for some alteration in what promised to be decades of fading routine until she and Almira and Emma dried into dust and blew away.

In the space of a month had come Aunt Maria's summons, Mr. Treffingham's endorsement of the trip, and all the frantic preparations. Now, at this moment, she was waterborne on her way to the future. An unpleasantness or two—the attack last night. But there were advantages too—as a prime example, Lord Lonsdale. He had come to be a large part of her life. They had spent time together making arrangements for the trip, and, in intervals during his occasional visits, enjoying each other's company. She had come some way since seeing him only infrequently and evanescently in her memory. Now she had more, much more, on which to build. Now she knew Justin himself, and not simply his strong features and his air of authority.

And three weeks ahead lay Vienna, and whatever pleasures would come to her there. And she would continue to see Justin. She dared not look any farther ahead—just to see Justin would be sufficient, for now.

Her mind drifted. How many queens had crossed

the Channel from Europe to England, to meet and
marry someone until then unknown? How many
times had England's kings crossed in the opposite
direction from Dover to Calais with armies of
longbowmen, crossbowmen, armored knights, even
war dogs encased in armor, and been sanguine of
success? And how many times had adversity been
their lot?

It did not do to plan ahead. But a good backing
wind gave cause for optimism—

"Fair stood the wind for France," came a famil-
iar voice in her ear, almost echoing her own thoughts.

Automatically, she continued the quotation. "When
we our sails advance,/ Nor now to prove our chance/
Longer will tarry."

Surprised, he said, "I had not thought anyone
read Drayton in these days."

"When one has a library at hand, and few dis-
tractions, one reads anything. My head is stuffed
with such oddments of learning, you may not
believe!"

"I wish you could enjoy the library at Plowden
Hall. I have become newly acquainted with it this
past fortnight."

"Your family seat, I collect?"

"Yes. My great-uncle, who held the title, attained
to such a vast age, however, that he discouraged
visitors, and I had not seen the place since I was a
boy."

They stood at the rail in companionable silence
for a moment. "The wind *is* fair," she commented.
"This could have put an army across in good time."

"Supposing, of course, that the ships could enter
Calais harbor, on a favorable tide."

"Is it possible that would not be the case?"

"I have known occasions when all the passengers,
still suffering acutely from *mal de mer,* would have

to disembark, climb down those little ladders into rowing boats, and then at the last be carried ashore by the watermen."

Her response to the thought of such a debacle was simple. "Good God. I should hate it."

He grinned. "I should imagine one would be more than grateful for a bit of solid land under one's feet, no matter how one reached it."

"Is there a chance of that this trip?"

"Probably not. The wind is fair, but the chop shows that it is due to change."

After a moment, he inquired, in an altered tone, "I am sorry you did not have opportunity to rest after your unfortunate incident last night. How do you feel this morning?"

"Nearly back to normal. I—I do not think I remembered to thank you for rescuing me last night. My wits were all abroad."

"No need to thank me. But I have wondered whether you have remembered anything more about your attacker?"

"N-no, I have not. There is something at the edge of my mind—I suppose that is why you questioned me so severely?"

"I thought you had not told me the whole, but I assumed that there were details you were not sure of at the time, and you would not speak hastily."

He knows me that well, she thought with an inner glow. "I would tell you if I could. But truly I cannot think why I would be attacked."

Hiding his amusement, he looked down at her. "Can't you?" He looked at her thin, intelligent face, the generous mobile mouth, the great hazel eyes of a clearness that a man might see through to eternity—then he brought himself up short. Was he a schoolboy to be taken with such juvenile fancies?

Suddenly self-conscious under his gaze, which

she considered stern, she turned away. She looked down at her ankle, and turned it, testing to see how sore it was. As she stood on one foot, uncertainly balanced, the ship lurched.

She clutched the air futilely. There was nothing to grab hold of. And for the second time in twenty-four hours, she was in his arms.

This time, she was not a limp, unconscious body. And this time, he lost his head.

The queer gnawing hunger that, not entirely known to him, he had thrust away, put out of mind in the interests of civility and knowing that since they would be spending weeks together he dared not stray from the paths of rectitude, now possessed him in a rush.

He held her tight, far longer than was necessary to restore her balance. She began to draw away, not from any disinclination to being held—in truth, she found her position excessively satisfactory—but merely as an automatic response to the dictates of propriety.

He did not release her. Pulling her even closer, he put a finger under her chin and tilted her face up to his. Gently, persuasively, he kissed her. At first her wits were numb—and then, with a warm, irresistible rush, she came alive. She lifted her arms and put them tightly around his neck, holding him. . . .

Some time later, immeasurable by ordinary mortals, she knew, she pulled away a short distance and looked up at him, her hazel eyes great with wonder.

He was white and shaken. He had not expected such sweetness ever to come into his life. Nor had he expected, if truth be told, to lose control of himself in such a total and devastating way.

She did not see in his face the assurance she

hoped for. With a great sigh she pulled out of his arms, and made a half-turn away from him.

So little had happened in that moment of time—and yet so much that she would never be quite the same Corinna. To her great surprise, she saw that the slate-colored waves still marched along the ship toward the stern, the sails overhead still stood out stiffly in the strong breeze. How could she have behaved in such a shameful manner? It was the result of that odd emotion that had swept her, and that she did not understand. Whatever it was, it boded no good for her.

Justin, seeing her standing apart from him, felt bereft. There was so much to say to her, so much to tell her. He believed it was not time yet to tell her he loved her, since they would be in company together on the road for the better part of a month. He would not place her in any kind of questionable position during the journey. But still his need to tell her, to bind her to him, was urgent.

What he would have said at that moment was to go forever unspoken.

"Corinna, there you are!" Emma Sanford was approaching them, nearly at a run. She looked briefly, but speculatively, from one to the other, but her errand was urgent. "Can you help me, my dear? Both of them are excessively ill and I do not quite see how I can manage."

"Of course," said Corinna swiftly. She glanced at Justin, an expression in her eyes he could not decipher, and with a whirl of her skirts followed Emma to the hatchway.

Turning back to the sea, Justin tried to collect his thoughts. Again lines from Drayton ran through his mind.

"Since there's no help, come let us kiss and part,/ Nay I have done: you get no more of me. . . ."

Please God, he thought fervently, that it never comes to that, for I think I am quite undone!

Justin and Francis accompanied Miss Morland and her party from Calais to Paris. Even the most rigid of duennas could not fault Lord Lonsdale and Mr. Ferrington for their exceedingly formal behavior toward the three ladies under their escort.

While Justin had his own reasons for stepping back from his first and heartfelt advance to Corinna, he did not share them with her. Indeed, it would have been impossible for him to confide in anyone but Francis.

The truth of the matter was that Napoleon, the conquered, was restless on Elba. Talleyrand and Wellington had both fought for the idea of placing Napoleon a few thousand miles farther away from the coast of France. However, the powers chose Elba. Now the allies kept close watch on the Corsican. Ostensibly, Sir Neil Campbell was merely the former emperor's liaison with the allies, but in truth he was enjoined to report Napoleon's slightest movement.

Nor were Sir Neil's the only pair of eyes watching Bonaparte. The Oil Merchant (a French secret agent on Elba reporting to Mariotti at Livorno) and a certain prefect of a district near Marseilles were also alert. Napoleon had never made a secret of his expectation of returning with the flowers of springtime—his favorite violets—to France, or, more probably, to somewhere on the Italian peninsula, where he had strong family interests.

The word Francis brought to Justin at Dover had come by devious ways along paths well worn by Justin's previous intelligence agents.

Since Justin was still officially attached to the staff of the Duke of Wellington, a summons to report to him at the embassy in Paris could not be ignored. Probably Boney had escaped—at least Francis said that was the current *on dit*. Justin could not pursue his own happiness until he found out what the duke wished of him.

Of course, Justin could not discuss military secrets with Corinna. He arranged in Paris for her and Miss Morland to join another quite large party traveling to Vienna, and sent her only a cryptic note, telling her that "circumstances beyond my control require my presence elsewhere."

The note was cold comfort. Corinna went over and over all the things that had occurred between her and Justin since she had fallen from the stile into his arms. Over and over—and the pivotal point, she was sure, was that wonderful, magical moment on the packet boat when he had kissed her. Previous to that moment they had been on friendly, not to say easy, terms. Following that moment, she had seen almost nothing of him.

I am not one, she thought to herself, to ignore a plain hint. A very plain hint. He was carried away by the moment and regrets it. Well, she added with a lift of her chin, no more than I do. He doesn't want any entanglements, that's clear. As though I would consider that he owed me anything. After all, what is a kiss?

Oddly, at this point she always felt the tears prickling at the back of her eyelids and was forced to think strongly of something else. Angry with Justin she certainly was. But she was also ashamed of her own response to him—not in the least passive.

The journey to Vienna was tedious. Almira was fretful and demanding, and Emma with great difficulty managed to cope without taking the girl by the shoulders and shaking her as a puppy shakes a rag. Corinna's own preoccupation prevented her from being much help to Emma.

Later, all she could remember of the journey was one vast sea of plain German inns, hot German stoves, stifling featherbeds, and one long progression of meals consisting of gingerbread with Branntwein or greasy black sausage with sauerkraut, either served with atrocious wine. But at least no one had to sleep overnight in the stables, as often happened.

Snow had begun to fall by the time they crossed the Danube and at last caught their first glimpse of Vienna.

The snow was thick enough to give the wooded hills a layer of white like cake icing. St. Stephen's spire was the first landmark they could distinguish. Its dainty fretwork held the snow like a dainty finger pointing up into the gray sky.

"Now at last I feel as though we were in a foreign land."

"Don't Germany and France count?"

"Foreign but not attractive. Now this is like opening a door to fairyland."

So it was. All their fatigue seemed to vanish in the excitement of one sight after another—the palaces, the Hofburg upon the hill, the enormous buildings, the place where the Lippizaner horses were trained.

The capital was so well endowed with palaces that each of the visiting national delegations was furnished one for its use. The duchess was housed, not as one might have expected in the English quarters, but in the Kaunitz Palace allocated to Prince Talleyrand.

"I wonder how she managed this," wondered Emma.

Corinna had little doubt. "She made a nuisance of herself until it was easier to give in than to continue protesting."

Emma, who remembered the duchess's visit to Morland Hall which resulted in the family rift, agreed. "I shall take care not to cross her in any way."

"If we are not forced into some havey-cavey scheme and lose our reputations," said Corinna darkly to Emma, "we may count ourselves fortunate indeed."

CHAPTER 11

Corinna's first meeting with the Duchesse de Carignac was all that she feared it would be, and worse.

Corinna had barely met the fearsome lady before, since on the occasion of the duchess's last visit to Morland Hall, she herself had been grieving sorely after her mother's death.

Now she recollected enough of her mother's shy confidences to suspect that Almira's aunt was headstrong at best, and fanatically fond of having her own way. Although Justin had said nothing to the point, yet she gathered from his manner that one found life easier if one simply went along with her wishes. It had been clear that he did not want to take back to the duchess the message that Almira did not choose to come when summoned.

Thus, at this moment of arrival in Vienna, the gayest capital in Europe, Corinna's heart began to sink. Perhaps the duchess would have forgotten her quarrel, perhaps she had mellowed in the intervening four years, perhaps—

At any rate, alighting at the carriage entrance of the grand Kaunitz Palace, allocated to the use of the French delegation to the peace conference, Corinna rallied her spirits. Surely, even though the duchess had not included her in her summons to Almira, she could not in all decency insult her.

A guide was found to escort the three ladies and a very nervous maid through the endless succession of public rooms on the ground floor of the Kaunitz. A grand staircase rose from a vast, marble-floored reception room, and the guide led the way up the stairs and then took the left arm of the stairs. Tucked away in a far corner of the second floor was a suite of rooms that the prince had allocated to the duchess, perhaps on the principle that it was easier to provide rooms for her than it was to listen to her constant complaints and petitions, at which form of intimidation she was an expert.

Not that the duchess had given up complaining, not at all.

Corinna's first sight of the duchess was a shocking one. The room into which they were ushered, after a short delay while the maid, Hannah, consulted with her mistress, was of good size, with tall windows looking out into parkland, and stifling hot.

Corinna's first impression was one of overwhelming furniture. There was not a square foot of carpet showing unimpeded by legs of little tables, taborets, chairs, sofas, ottomans. Corinna looked around her curiously, while Almira greeted her aunt. Her eye was caught by the astounding objects on the square galleried table next to the duchess's settee.

Although she could not take them all in at once, she later decided that the jewels, laid out on the table for the duchess to enjoy, must constitute a vast fortune.

There was one ruby-and-diamond necklace, the pendant set with a cushion-cut diamond as big as a hazelnut, surrounded by at least eight magnificent rubies, attached to a chain of diamonds. And an old-fashioned tiara—the same, although she did not know it, that Justin had noted. Lost in admiration of a sapphire-and-emerald brooch set in yellow gold filigree, she did not at first hear that the duchess was speaking to her.

"Aha, Miss Darley. I wondered what you could have come all the way to Vienna for."

Corinna was a firm believer in beginning as one means to go on. "Because I would not send my stepsister alone," she said firmly, trying not to stare at the duchess.

For the Duchesse de Carignac was quite the stoutest woman Corinna had ever seen. She half sat, half lay on the settee, since no chair could have encompassed her great size. Her face, overly powdered and—Corinna suspected—not overly clean either, was wide as a full moon, with little black eyes that were nearly lost in folds of flesh.

"I did not invite you," the duchess said abruptly. "I no longer wonder why you came. If you are like your mother, and you do resemble her mightily—a pity—you came to see what you can get out of me. Well, I take leave to tell you that not one cent will you get from me."

"Ma'am, I do not wish—"

"Don't interrupt me. I can see you staring at those jewels. My jewels, if you please."

Suppressing anger, Corinna said, "I only wondered whether it was wise to have such a great number of valuable stones on display."

The duchess gave way to a kind of explosion, which Corinna correctly diagnosed as laughter. "I like to have my little baubles where I can see them. Hannah gets them out every day for me." Eying Corinna carefully, as though to decide where to send the next dart, she added deliberately, "I suppose for someone who never had anything, these must look like a vast fortune. I assure you, they are nothing."

In comparison to what? Corinna wondered. But

she was too incensed to respond to the duchess's insults, and after a moment, the latter turned to her niece.

"You took your time in getting here, Almira."

"I am sorry, Aunt Maria," said Almira, bearing up bravely. "There was so much to do to get ready to come."

"Nonsense. What could a slip of a girl like you have to do? I'd be much surprised if you do as much as choose what gown you wear. No, don't gammon me, my girl. Miss Darley ought to earn her keep some way."

"But I do not keep her, aunt."

"Don't trouble me with whatever excuses you may have in your mind. Tell me about your journey. Was Lord Lonsdale gallant?"

Almira was exhibiting signs of restless rebellion at her aunt's inquisition, and Miss Sanford thought it best to come to Almira's rescue. "Lord Lonsdale is the epitome of elegance." Cunningly she added, "Am I correct, ma'am, in believing him related to you?"

The duchess was pleased with Miss Sanford. "Yes, indeed you are. My first husband was a Ferrington, you know, and although he did not have the title—dear Justin has that—all that family are enormously wealthy." She waved a hand negligently toward the jewels on the table. "But," she resumed, "I must say I am greatly displeased with Francis."

"Francis?" echoed Almira, who had taken a liking to him. "How can that be?"

"He did not see fit to inform me as to when you would arrive. I am certain he must have known, for Justin dotes on the boy, oddly enough. But Francis did not even send me a note, and he must have known I would wish to know."

Almira's awe of her Aunt Maria, rather than fading, had grown stronger. But she entertained an admiration for Francis, whom she liked much better than Lord Lonsdale, and, though stumbling over the words, protested. "I do not understand, Aunt. Why should Lord Lonsdale inform Francis, when Francis was with him?"

The question, simple as it was, yet brought the duchess to a state of speechlessness. "Francis? With you? I did not know that." Probably, thought Corinna, she was uneasy over any circumstance she did not control. Fretfully, at last she said, "He should have told me. Who do they think I am, that they can ignore me? I am very close to Prince Talleyrand, and when I receive the de Carignac lands back in my own hands, I will—well, never mind what I will do. But young Francis will be sorry enough that he did not inform me." She fixed Almira with a hard glare. "I suppose that Francis made much over you?"

Sensing that even a truthful answer—that he had merely watched Almira from a respectful distance— would not serve, Corinna explained smoothly, "We were forced to linger in Paris for several days—"

"In God's name, why? Paris is a dead city compared to Vienna."

"Lord Lonsdale thought we would be safer in the company of a group of English persons who were about to start for Vienna."

"He did, eh?"

This interrogation had gone on long enough, so Corinna deemed. Suddenly the long days of bouncing, rugged riding, of stale pent-up carriage air and musty, airless inn rooms, the digestive upsets caused by an endless array of greasy food and sleepless nights, all descended upon her at once. She would have given half her fortune—such as it was—for a bed with clean sheets, a small crackling fire on the hearth, and a steaming cup of tea.

Since she was already in the duchess's black looks, one more irritation could not matter. "Where are we to lodge, ma'am? I confess to being very weary."

The duchess snorted. "I am not at all surprised. As you grow older, the slightest discomfort takes its toll." She favored Corinna with a look of contempt. "I am not surprised you didn't take."

Temper, temper! Corinna could almost hear her mother's warning voice. "You may remember, ma'am, that I was called home after only a short time in London."

The duchess could not resist the opportunity afforded. "Of course. Your family stock is weak." Then, answering Corinna's question, she added, "You will stay next door to my own suite. Hannah will show you." Turning to her niece, she said, "I will be of great help to you, teaching you how to go on."

"I'm most grateful."

"As you should be. I am persuaded you will need much tutoring, for you will be moving in the highest of circles. I should not at all be surprised were an ambassadorship in the offing. The dear duke—Wellington, of course, I mean—will be chivvied out of Paris at the first opportunity. You know the French loathe him. And I have some little influence, you know. Yes, there could indeed be an embassy in the offing. What would you say, child, to starting your married life at the top of society?"

"Married life?" echoed Almira, in such a small voice that she merely mouthed the words.

"Marriage?" asked Corinna.

"Of course. Why else would I have sent for her? I have a great match in mind for my niece."

Corinna persisted. "Does Mr. Treffingham know?"

The duchess was instantly indignant. "Who is he? What has he to do with anything? I am the child's only relative, don't forget that. And I arrange her marriage."

"Is it already arranged, then?"

"It's none of your affair," said the duchess crossly. Then, possibly stirred by an irrepressible urge to boast, she said, "Perhaps not precisely *arranged*. Nothing signed, of course. But after all, the man has been in your company for several weeks, and I make no doubt that within hours he'll be in here to talk to me. You are a beauty, child, and even though your mother's looks faded, they were enough to get her a husband. You'll do the same."

"But I do not wish to be married," protested Almira. "At least—not to a stranger."

The duchess laughed, and Corinna could not refrain from thinking that there was more evil in the sound than there was amusement. "A brilliant match, my girl. A Ferrington connection can't be bettered."

"Ferrington?" echoed Almira.

"But he's much too young," protested Corinna.

The duchess gave her a sharp look. "Nonsense. I don't know what you mean, too young. Besides, ages do not matter. It is the connection that is important. The Ferringtons are wealthy as nabobs. Don't ever think that I do not have the family's interests in mind. At bottom, it's up to me to marry you off, and so I will."

Corinna, bravely, protested again. "But surely you are moving too quickly on this, ma'am. Almira must see something of the world first."

"Of course, young Miss Interfering. But she'll see the world here in Vienna, and go home a married woman. What more could she want?" The duchess beamed upon them, immensely pleased with her own arrangements.

"But," insisted Corinna, "he has not come into his majority. I cannot conceive of anything more ill-advised." She had thought she spoke aloud, but when the room did not explode, she realized that she had merely protested in her mind.

The protest, however, was real enough. There were so many facets to the proposed marriage, it could not be possible for the duchess to consider them all. In truth, Corinna thought ruefully, the duchess cared nothing for complications or for anyone's feelings. She herself had wounds to prove the duchess's cruelty.

First of all, there were Almira's penchants to deal with. She had been infatuated with Jack Hardie to a degree that Corinna had not been aware of. Jack was now in the past, for how could a great but juvenile love maintain itself over a separation of a thousand miles? But who was to say that Almira might not entertain a *tendre* for the next young man she saw, and the one after that?

Almira was capable, so Corinna surmised, of cutting a wide but inconstant swath through all the minor counts and dukes of the Vienna scene. With the czar's vast household also staying in Vienna, as well as Castlereagh's mission, the arena for the effects of Almira's beauty was broadened greatly.

And Francis himself—he was an admirer of Almira's, of course; who wouldn't be? But was he serious? Corinna could not recall any sign of an inordinate attachment on the part of either of the young people. All these objections flew through Corinna's thoughts on swift wings, and, at the end, she thought again that the duchess was greatly ill-advised.

She heard, as though an echo of her own thoughts,

Almira's voice, saying on an odd note, "Does Francis know?"

The duchess glared at her. "What has he to do with the matter? Francis is just a young cub. The marriage"—and here the duchess's optimism slipped into falsehood—"the marriage I have arranged is with Justin. Lord Lonsdale, my child! *He's* your future husband!"

CHAPTER 12

In another part of the city, Justin had no thought of marriage on his mind, at least in the forefront. Europe had just emerged from two decades of French upheaval, and Justin had a strong feeling that the trouble was not finished. Much as, he thought, a serpent twitches dangerously even while dying.

Having been delayed for several days at the Iron Duke's behest in Paris, he finally arrived in Vienna, and he hastened to the palace occupied by the English delegation. His own rooms, kept for him, provided him the opportunity to clear away the stains of travel, and he was once again an elegant gentleman who gave no signs of having traveled over particularly unpleasant roads for some days.

Not that the journey had been without its points of entertainment, not at all. In the first place, he realized that he had come very near to queering his pitch for all time with the woman with whom he wished to spend the rest of his life. He had spent hours on the road going over as though with a magnifying lens every word she had spoken, every gesture she had made. He had been sure that she looked upon him with every kind of favor.

And for that reason, refining too much on his expectations, he had lost his head on the ferry. It was fate that threw her for the third time into his ready arms. He had been stirred on the first occasion, when she had tumbled from the stile to his feet. On the second, he had been worried out of his mind, fearing her dead from that villainous attack. The third time—the charm.

He had succumbed to what every well-bred young lady must term his baser instincts. Instinct it was, and it had propelled him into the most injudicious of actions—kissing his dear Corinna with unbridled passion. He frightened her away to such a distance that she had been cold as the snowbound German landscape he had later traversed.

He could not blame her. There had been one moment, on the packet, when he had thought she had responded to his passion, had pressed her delicious body closer to his, even embracing him with arms around his neck—

He was not sure, could not believe his good fortune if that had been the case.

He had to confer with Wellington in Paris, and his time was not his own. He particularly felt he must not travel day after day in her company, and spend night after dismal night in unsavory inns, with only a miss just out of the schoolroom and an indulgent lady's companion to serve as Corinna's chaperon. He was quite sure he could control himself, but already he felt he must protect her against all hazards, and even the appearance of impropriety must not be allowed.

Now, bearing news of moment from Wellington to Castlereagh, he followed the minister's secretary to the great room, possibly intended as a library, where Lord Castlereagh awaited him.

"This congress dances more than it works," exploded Castlereagh, after they were settled with brandy, "as the Prince de Ligne pointed out to me only the other day. There is a man with a flair for the apt phrase! Every man here—that is, the czar, the Emperor Francis, and we—has huge standing armies all over the map. Napoleon has so wrecked the former ruling families that it's impossible to come to terms with new boundaries, and the royals will accept nothing less than putting the clock back to the way it formerly was. And the principals!"

He took a turn around the room before he went on. "They are all tyrants! Despots, with all their whims, feuds, and ambitions, do nothing but muddle an already impossible situation. The czar, in particular, has become so capricious. . . ." Lord Castlereagh lowered his voice to a confidential murmur. "I think the man's mad. Family none too stable, you know. This Alexander played with soldiers as a lad."

Amused, Justin countered, "Doesn't every boy?"

"With *real* soldiers? Drilling and deploying them in old battles—just as though they were six inches high and made of tin!"

"Good God!"

"Just so. Often he tells us that his Cossacks had ridden to Paris and could as easily ride to Vienna and take this capital as well. He hates the Bourbons! Of course, I can understand that. Louis treated the czar shamefully, as though the Bourbon king had put the czar back on *his* throne, instead of the other way around. A stupid man!"

"Louis?" guessed Justin.

"Oh, no—both of them," pronounced Lord Castlereagh.

"I do recall that Lord Liverpool told the Duke of Wellington shortly before Christmas—was it a year ago?—the only sovereign in whom we can have any real confidence is the King of France."

"Even Metternich," resumed Castlereagh, filling

glasses again, "has lost his head for several weeks. Ever since his thwarted love affair with the Duchess of Sagan—sister to Talleyrand's niece, if that's what she is—absorbed him. But enough gossip. I'm getting as bad as an old woman. What news do you bring?"

"The duke is not popular in Paris. In truth, his life has been threatened. Sir Neil Campbell tells me that Napoleon's not receiving his pension. Believe me, this will lead to tragedy."

Castlereagh was unmoved. "It's up to the allies—not England—to fulfill their commitments to him. That is Alexander's duty. Otherwise, we will have him back on our hands."

"The Oil Merchant tells me revolution will break out in March."

"Well, perhaps we can settle him once and for all then. In the meantime, what of you? How did you fare in England? I admit I do not know precisely for what purpose you went."

"The Duchesse de Carignac sent me—it was a family errand."

Justin had nearly forgotten how resentful he had been over the duchess's high-handed manner in sending him to look after her niece, who after all was not in the least related to him.

However, his errand had brought him Corinna, and while he was reluctant to fix his interest with her until he could take her back with him to the Ferrington country seat, he still thought it possible that she would be his, at the right time. She had exhibited some tender feeling toward him, he felt, forgetting the occasions when she had not, and perhaps—could it really be?—she had even responded to his passionate embrace. He could not now think of Corinna without feeling—at least in memory—the packet deck rising beneath his feet, and his Corinna in his arms, her sweet lips moving beneath his own.

Castlereagh had been watching him with speculation in his eyes. "My dear Lonsdale," he ventured, "do I detect that you are about to be caught in parson's mousetrap?"

With a reluctant smile, Justin glossed over his abstraction. "Not so, sir. For I should not think it advisable to choose a wife from this higgledy-piggledy assortment of place-seekers and greedy high-flyers."

"Quite true," agreed the envoy. "But you must admit, the air is full of romance!"

"Full of malice, envy, and all uncharitableness," he said sourly, thinking of his cousin Maria. "I wish—although wishes come easily and without high cost—I wish that Napoleon would make his break out of Elba as soon as possible, so that we can meet his challenge and then remove him far out of sight and out of mind."

"You think he will really make a break for it? Sir Neil Campbell considers that even without the regular payment of his pension he is content where he is."

"Sir Neil is a fool, then. My man on Elba—"

"The Oil Merchant? I do not trust a man who will not reveal his name."

"In my late business, sir, names were not common currency," Justin pointed out dryly, and went on as though there had been no interruption,"—says that Bonaparte's pension has not been paid for a purpose. That the allies are setting a trap for Bonaparte."

Castlereagh's expression was enigmatic. Justin continued, "To make him think we are not to be trusted, and he may—on that sole account—break his bonds." Now Justin caught the sly satisfaction in Castlereagh's face.

"I see. Soon, then?"

"Our former foe was never a patient man. Besides, did he not promise his men he would return with the *fleurs de printemps?*"

"Spring flowers," mused Justin. "He was always partial to violets, I have heard. Well, then, perhaps we may conclude this business before the summer."

And then, he thought as he left Castlereagh's study, I will take Corinna back to England as soon as I can. If Cousin Maria carries out the duty she spoke so strongly about, she will have disposed of that simpleton Almira, and my Corinna will be free of her.

Justin planned to make a courtesy call on Corinna—and of course her companions—to inquire about their health, now that they were no longer on the road. A rigorous journey, even for him, and it would have been much more fatiguing for delicate ladies who were unused to travel.

But there were dispatches from his network of Napoleon-watchers, and invitations to a ball given by Czar Alexander that he must attend, and, while Corinna was not put out of his mind, yet there were insistent and clamorous items that demanded his immediate attention.

Francis was full of news. "I have been told, Justin, that one must not use one's wastepaper basket for waste paper."

Justin was startled. "What would one use it for, then?"

"The emperor gets a daily report on the town gossip, the letters, the pieces discarded—"

"I hope he gets his fill of corrected drafts of love

poems. Castlereagh is quite indignant about the surfeit of *amours* around us!"

Francis was silent for a moment. Then he said, in a way he hoped would sound casual, "I thought I would take Miss Morland for a drive tomorrow afternoon." His cousin was not deceived.

"Miss Morland, is it?" said Justin, an odd note in his voice.

"You object, do you?" said Francis irritably. "Don't tell me you have an interest there?"

"That beautiful idiot? Good God, no!"

"She is not an idiot!"

Surely there was more heat here than expected. "No? I must bow to your greater discernment, then."

"Well, I agree she is not well educated," said Francis, reasonably avoiding a quarrel with Justin. "Nor does she have much experience in the world. But she has not had the steadiness in her life that would be the making of her."

Justin gave him a level measuring stare. "And you will provide such steadiness?"

"Perhaps, although I am not sure as I was that she is worth parson's mousetrap. Besides, from something I heard her say on the journey, I fear she has another in mind."

"Surely you do not consider her wishes as a serious, immutable decision? Better believe a weathercock in March. If she does have an interest, it can only be in that Hardie boy. She knows no one else."

Francis agreed. "That is why I do not wish to move too quickly, Justin. I should not wish her to choose me for lack of knowing anyone else."

"I daresay you are right," said Justin, his interest in Miss Morland waning swiftly. "But there is plenty of time. We are thousands of miles from Gretna Green, so I assume the lady will stay where she is for a time. But to keep you from fatal ennui while Miss Morland embarks upon society, I wish you to look over these dispatches, and tell me how soon you think Boney will leave his island kingdom behind.''

CHAPTER 13

The duchess may daily have required her faithful but grumbling Hannah to remove her several caskets of jewels from the hiding place she had devised and spread the various items on the table beside her sofa, but she had no intention of allowing any of them out of her hands.

Particularly was she determined not to spend her own money if not positively forced to do so, though she wished for Almira a splendid ball to introduce her to society, so that she would show off to best advantage in the eyes of Justin Ferrington.

An impartial observer might have wondered why the duchess was determined to marry her niece to Lord Lonsdale, since he was nearly fifteen years older and as sophisticated a man of the world as could be found. Even though not privy to the inner workings of the duchess's mind—she wished to gather both Justin's vast wealth and his French influence into her hands, with an eye on her own advantage—an onlooker would be forced reluctantly to admire the devious way she set about getting her wishes.

"The dear prince," she informed Corinna and Almira, a day or two after their arrival, "has most graciously allowed us rooms in his palace. Although the Kaunitz Palace is not the Belvedere, yet it is spacious and roomy, and Talleyrand's cook is su-

perb. He brought Carème from Paris, you know. I
vow I have never enjoyed such cuisine."

Corinna's mind wandered. She realized she had
developed an uncivil habit of not listening to what
the duchess might say, having decided that Maria
Morland was less intelligent than her brother, and
that Sir Rupert came out far better in the area of
kindness.

Corinna had much on her mind. She had, as it
were, cherished Justin in her dreams these two
years. She had known that logically she must be a
fool, for there was not a chance in a thousand that
she would ever exchange a word with him. But
truly there had been no one else to make up the
stuff of dreams. Certainly Mr. Willoughby was not
tinder for that flame. She had not "taken" in her
truncated season, and while a marriage might have
been arranged for her, Sir Rupert was so distracted
by her mother's illness and death that he gave his
stepdaughter no attention. Corinna was resigned
enough to stay at Morland Hall, dreading another
London failure.

But now the unexpected, unimaginable event had
occurred, and Justin had appeared in her life. She
lingered over the conversations they had enjoyed at
Morland Hall, over his rescue of her at Dover, and
his obvious concern for her.

And that long moment on the packet boat—that
came again and again to her, and this time not in
dreams. Wide awake she was, and she remembered
every slightest detail—his hand on her shoulder,
his fingers lifting her face to his, her instinctive
movement closer to him, pressing her body against
his—

"You're not listening, Corinna!" came the duchess's harsh voice. "When I speak, you are to pay
attention to me."

"Yes, ma'am," said Corinna submissively, seeing in her mind's eye the fragments of memory lying broken around her feet.

"We may expect the Princesse de Courland, any moment," said the duchess with an air of sly triumph. "Her uncle, Talleyrand, is sending her. He wishes to honor me by giving my niece a ball to introduce her. I am sure we may leave all the details in the princess's hands."

Almira was subdued, as she had been since arriving in Vienna. Corinna was so stunned by the duchess's plans for her stepsister—marrying her to Justin, who had not hesitated to engage Corinna's interest—that she had overlooked the unusual attitude of her stepsister. At home, Almira would be throwing vases if she was thwarted, or riding out for hours without explaining her absences.

Corinna looked curiously at Almira now. The suggestion of a ball should have raised the girl to near ecstasy, but she appeared to think that her doom had just been pronounced.

"The Princesse de Courland?" said Corinna politely, seeing that Almira was lost to the duty of making conversation. "I have heard her name mentioned."

"All lies!" said the duchess softly. "She is my good friend, and I will hear no scandal about her." She gave a sly, unpleasant wink at Corinna. "There is more than one way to accomplish one's ends. If justice is lacking, then subterfuge must take its place."

"I don't understand," Almira said. "I don't understand anything about why we are here in Vienna."

"Because the allied powers are dealing with the mess Bonaparte made of Europe!" exploded the duchess. "And they are deciding what to do with France, whether to carve it up or put that idiotic

Bourbon king away again, or who knows what they have in their minds."

"But," said Almira, exhibiting the stubbornness that was one of her least attractive qualities, "what has that to do with me?"

The duchess glared at Corinna. "Haven't you taught her anything?"

Corinna had an uncertain grasp on her own temper, but for once she was not angry with Almira. "What my stepsister says, ma'am, makes good sense to me. I cannot see why we have been dragged on an unpleasant journey in midwinter, simply to go to a ball in Vienna."

She knew she was making her objection in the simplest terms, but she could not explain all the complex currents that eddied in her mind, even if she had wanted to.

"I told you. She is to marry Lord Lonsdale."

Corinna swallowed hard. "That marriage could have been arranged in England, and we would all have been much more comfortable." Belatedly, diplomacy returned to her. "And you would not have had to put yourself out so greatly for us."

"I cannot leave Vienna. That should be apparent even to you. Not until I get my estates back. The prince is far too busy to deal with my affairs at the moment, but I have great hopes of his niece. I have made a great friend of her, and we are in each other's pockets."

"Only fancy," murmured Corinna. "I have heard much to her detriment in only the short time I have been here."

She was rewarded by a daggerlike glare from the duchess. What she might have said was never uttered, for Hannah threw the door to the small salon open and announced, "Her highness the Princesse de Courland."

Dorothée de Courland had married, under protest and unhappily, Edmond de Pérogord, Talleyrand's nephew. Summoned by Talleyrand to serve as his hostess in Vienna, Dorothée was, perhaps for the first time in her life, approaching happiness.

She was thin to the point of angularity, and dark-skinned. Her eyes, however, were magnificent. At first Corinna thought they were as black as her hair, but they were deep violet, and exceptionally expressive. Corinna did not realize, as she looked for a moment into those smoldering eyes, that she had just had a unique experience.

Instantly, the princess looked away, as though withdrawing to a harbor within her, and her lips curled in her habitual expression of contempt. It was well known that Dorothée never allowed a meeting of eyes.

It may have been the burning violet eyes, or it may have been something more intangible and yet personal, but Corinna could not take her eyes off the visitor. Dorothée sat without invitation and acknowledged introductions with a languid, careless air. She did not try to hide her thoughts. She glanced at Almira for a moment, as one might notice a porcelain shepherdess, and passed her by. To the duchess's disgust, Dorothée clearly considered Almira as not worth her trouble.

But she turned to Corinna, and examined her more carefully. Then she smiled, a brief flash of light as of sun breaking through clouds.

"Are you feeling quite at home here? I collect that the politics of this congress are of little interest to you, as they would be for me, except that my uncle does talk a good deal."

With surprising pains, Dorothée set herself to drawing Corinna out, on books, on music, even on her hopes of finding a husband in Vienna.

"I think not," said Corinna gently. A large lie was no harder to speak than a little lie, so she added, "There is no one I have seen that I could fancy."

She knew she had spoiled it all by blushing, a faint warm pink that climbed from her throat into her cheeks. Dorothée's sharp eyes did not miss the telltale sign.

Fascinated by the possibility of intrigue, and oddly attracted by the intelligence she discovered in Corinna, she suggested, as she rose to take her departure, "Miss Darley, perhaps you will come to tea with me, tomorrow afternoon, and we can talk further."

"How nice of you, your highness!" exclaimed the duchess. "We will be delighted to come."

Corinna caught her breath. Already she knew the princess well enough to suspect that, in her exalted position, she feared nothing and nobody, and in all likelihood used her tongue freely for her own amusement. The duchess had pointedly not been included in the invitation.

The princess turned to look directly at the duchess, and said, her voice chilled by contempt, *"We?"*

Corinna stiffened. The slight movement must have caught the princess's eye, for she added, in a careless voice, "I am sorry, but I do recall an urgent engagement for tomorrow afternoon. Perhaps another time."

The crisis was past, for the moment.

"Come, Miss Darley," she said, "pray escort me to the door."

Nothing was said until the princess was outside in the corridor, and Corinna stood in the doorway to the duchess's suite. The duchess and Almira remained in the small salon, but Corinna suspected they were both straining their ears to listen.

"Miss Darley, a word of advice."

"Yes, your highness?"

"Don't be misled by all the glitter here in Vienna. Don't do as I did—marry for someone else's convenience. It leads to the greatest unhappiness in the world. Imagine being forced to live with a man of the shallowest interests, whose main occupation is gambling, and who has an eye to any woman but his wife."

Corinna, moved by the apparent misery in the woman's aristocratic features, reached out to touch her, but remembered in time the difference between their stations. "But," said Corinna, surprising herself, and thinking of her own conservative means, "is it not better to marry, even to be neglected, than to live for forty years as a constrained spinster with barely enough money to keep two servants and a carriage?"

The princess gave her a lopsided smile. "Jewels are the answer, my dear. And don't tell me you have none. I am sure you don't. Acquire some."

Bewildered, Corinna said, "But how?"

"A husband is not the only man who may have jewels to shower on you." She nodded in the direction of the salon. "The duchess did marry hers. But marriage is a serious step, and irrevocable. Jewels are mere material objects—but there is great power in their possession. Freedom is worth any sacrifice."

Corinna, even as new to Vienna as she was, had a strong sense of rarity. The interview she was having with the Princesse de Courland, while not unusual between good friends, was unparalleled in the brittle, highly charged atmosphere of the capital. And yet, she could not suspect Dorothée of being insincere.

"Too bad our lives have crossed too late," Dorothée said soberly to Corinna. "Your upbringing, which

must have been without great amusements, had a
certain stability which I envy."

Corinna smiled wryly. "You envy me? I cannot
accept that. For I long to have your address, your
worldly intelligence—I confess I often do not know
how to go on." She looked away, for the emotion of
the moment threatened to undo her. She could feel
her lower lip beginning to tremble.

"You see?" Dorothée pointed out. "We could have
helped each other, if we had met in time."

There was a small pause, both reluctant to sepa-
rate. Corinna found words first. "It is so good of
your uncle to bring my stepsister into society with
a ball."

Dorothée laughed, a short bark of sound. "Is that
what she told you? My dear, you must not believe
all you hear. In Vienna, I would guess that one
word out of ten is genuine."

Corinna was shocked at the duchess's lie, but yet
on another level she was not surprised. "Then
why—?"

"Whatever reason she gives, at base there is only
one reason. Advantage to herself. I must ask my
uncle why he does not send her away."

A call from within broke their mood. "Shut that
door, Corinna! There's a great draft!"

Dorothée took Corinna's hands. "In another world
we might have been friends."

Corinna, both attracted and repelled by this an-
gular, monkey-faced woman without apparent charm
and yet with an irresistible magnetism, said simply, "I would have liked that."

The princess lowered her voice so that those in
the inner room could not hear. "My dear, if you
ever think that I can help you, please do not fail to
come to me."

Corinna, greatly daring, murmured, "One word in ten?"

"I was not mistaken in you," laughed the princess. "In my case, at this moment, ten words in ten."

The duchess was disgruntled, and made no secret of it. "Whatever that woman told you, Corinna, you must put out of your mind. She is a dissolute woman, as are her two sisters and her mother. The Duchess of Sagan leads Metternich by the nose. Those women will sleep in any bed that's nearby, and not alone, either."

Corinna protested. "Almira is not used to such— frankness." *Vulgarity*, not to put too fine a point to it.

"Then she had better become accustomed, for I wish her to outshine every woman in Vienna. Look at her! Such a beauty you never saw before. That woman going on about jewels—she has to, for she has the ugliest face I ever saw!"

Later, alone in the room she shared with Almira, Corinna repeated to herself Dorothée's advice. "Marriage is a straitjacket, and wealth is for the taking—or more accurately, I suppose, the giving."

Justin was to marry Almira, the duchess had said. It was all arranged, but for the moment kept secret. Justin had quite clearly no intention of considering his marriage a straitjacket—witness the very friendly interest he had exhibited as far as Corinna herself was concerned. Now that she thought about it—and as strongly as that moment on the packet came back to her—it was not his touch alone that stirred her. It was his intelligence, his broad education, and his willingness to laugh. There had been little enough laughter in her life, for her mother had been ill, and Sir Rupert, essentially a stupid man, had been wary of levity.

I have no intention, she told herself, of behaving with impropriety. I am not a princess with powerful relatives, to carry off any scandal.

And yet, after Almira marries Justin, who would care if I did? No one in this world!

CHAPTER 14

The Talleyrand ball, while not given either to honor the duchess or to celebrate Almira's arrival in Vienna, nonetheless occurred in due course. In truth, all of Vienna was one large party.

If one believed rumor—even at the rate of one genuine word in ten—there was little virtue at the congress. Corinna was told that earlier that fall, after only ten days of deliberations in October, the members of the congress declared a recess of three weeks to catch up on their social obligations.

It was true that there were only two things to do in Vienna, and one of them was spying. Official duties claimed only a small number of the tremendous number of strangers crammed into the city. Palaces and hovels alike were in demand at astronomical prices. The walls had ears, and every word was repeated, weighed, and repeated again by someone, somewhere in the city.

Until the powers agreed on the main questions, there could be no promises made nor accord reached on the myriad of smaller points.

Talleyrand, of course, was a prime object of intrigue, one of the most influential and powerful men at the congress. His every thought was suspect. The Austrian police particularly were baffled by the French minister, primarily because they could detect his hand in no intrigues whatever. Surely, they thought, he must have spies and agents, for everyone else was enmeshed in conspiracy to the eyebrows.

"Can you believe," said Emma in some indignation, "they even suspect Neukomm? The pianist, you know."

"I have heard a few notes of music coming from the main wing, quite late at night. Is your Neukomm responsible?" said Corinna, brushing her dark blond hair.

"Not my Neukomm. But I am drawn to listen, and the servants allow me to sit quietly in an anteroom, while Monsieur Neukomm soothes the prince. The prince claims he thinks better to music. And such magnificent playing! I am quite transported by it."

"You know him? I am not surprised that you have made his acquaintance, for I know your love of music." She was intrigued to note a slight flush on Emma's cheeks. "And not only the music, but perhaps the musician?"

Emma frowned. "I don't know what's gotten into me, Corinna. Vienna may look like a fairyland, but there is only dirt and squalidness underneath the surface. But there is something about the place that sets my reason to one side. I cannot think straight anymore. I know I should be with Almira, but she is gone much of the time, and knowing she is with you, I have forgotten her."

Corinna paused in her rhythmic stroking. "With me? Once in a sennight, perhaps, no more. I had thought she was with you."

They stared at each other. "What can this mean?" ventured Emma.

"I cannot think," said Corinna stoutly, after a moment of reflection, "that Almira is doing anything improper. Indeed, I would suspect that she is for the most part in the company of Lord Lonsdale. After all, the duchess says they are all but affianced."

"Of course. That must be it," agreed Emma, but her frown did not go away. She had seen no signs of attachment in either party. "Although since the betrothal is not public, perhaps one of us should warn her that it is improper to be seen too often in his company."

"Emma, my dear, I have the oddest notion that here in Vienna all the rules we lived by at home have been abandoned. That no one cares for appearances, even for decency."

Emma nodded wisely. "The princess has persuaded you to her way of thinking?"

"No, she has not. We have spent time together, but not, I assure you, discussing morality. I should not think her views would be edifying!"

"I have not liked to say this," said Emma, "but I wonder whether she is not a disturbing influence. You have not been yourself this fortnight, ever since we first saw the duchess. I will agree with whatever vulgar names you wish to call her, but you must admit that she is doing her best for Almira."

Almira to be Lady Lonsdale! Even though Almira did not appear overjoyed at the prospect, quite certainly it was the best that could be done for her. To think of Almira settled—and so well—at last, and no longer a heavy responsibility of Corinna's! Corinna must rejoice at it.

Corinna, however, was wretched. She would have given any sum to know that such an arrangement was not true.

Nellie tapped on the door then, and in a moment Almira was forgotten in the hurry to dress for the ball.

Later that evening, the duchess, supported by

two canes and the dour Hannah, led Almira, Corinna, and Emma to be presented to their host.

Talleyrand—who was by now an elderly weary man save for the sharp piercing intelligence in his eyes—sat on a sofa to receive his guests. Beside him sat his nephew's wife, Dorothée, mysterious and dazzlingly ugly, and wonderfully elegant. She wore a fortune in jewels, but in spite of their outrageous size, they did not appear gaudy.

She grinned at Corinna, who recalled the princess's advice to acquire gems, no matter how. Making a slight gesture toward her jewels, she murmured, truthfully as it happened, "My mother gave them to me."

The company was the most glittering in Europe, more kings than one could count, two emperors, princes and archdukes, and Corinna, after making her curtsy to her host and hostess, moved away on the arm of a count whose name she never learned.

There was music, and there was a murmuring of voices rising and falling like the surf on the shore. There was an overpowering mixture of scents, worn both by men and women, and Corinna, accustomed to the simple fresh smells of the country, and quiet rural sounds, felt her head beginning to throb.

She watched the Czar of All the Russias, a handsome and arrogant man, lead his currently favorite lady—but never the Czarina Elizabeth, whom for the most part he ignored—onto the floor in the first steps of the stately polonaise, the new dance that was the rage now.

Over the shoulders of her own partner, she searched the crowd looking for one face. She found it. Justin was leading Almira through the complicated dance, apparently oblivious to the mutinous expression on her beautiful face.

Corinna had partners in plenty, and she did love

to dance, but the evening wore on, a blurred succession of hours that Corinna thought would never end. When a new gentleman appeared and dismissed her escort of the moment, she drew a deep breath and prepared for the next set.

When he did not move, she looked into his face. "Justin! I did not expect you."

"I can see that. But I think I arrived at a fortunate moment. We shall not dance." In a burst, he exploded, "I have never seen you so tired! Could one of these oafs not bring you some refreshment?"

"I think one started to," she said vaguely—how delightful it was to hear the concern in Justin's voice! "But he never came back."

"I can do better than that." He grinned. "Let us go to that small sofa between the windows."

She sat at last with a heartfelt sigh. She regarded the toe of her slipper doubtfully. It peeked out from beneath her brocade skirt, and there was without doubt a black streak across the green silk.

"One of your more cumbersome friends?" said Justin lightly.

"Do you know, I do not know the name of one gentleman who danced with me? Such a crush!"

Justin indeed did better than her erstwhile companion, for he waylaid a servant who returned in moments with champagne.

It was not only the wine, she thought somewhat later, that caused the oddest constriction in the region of her heart. Even though Justin sat with a careful and obvious space between them, she was suffocatingly aware of him. Had she truly pressed herself against the whole length of his hard-muscled body? Yes, she had, and she would do it again if he touched her. Such a notion! She was becoming as depraved as the rest of Viennese society.

Sobering, she set herself to listen to Justin's diverting and clever sketches of certain of the crowd. The Princess Bagration, primary but not exclusive mistress of the czar and a born *intrigante*. The Czarina Elizabeth, blond and blue-eyed, who had rebelled against joining her husband in France since she would have to be civil to persons she thought beneath her. Her dislike of plebeian crowds was well known, and her dislike of her husband not quite so obvious, except for the constant presence by her side of Prince Adam Czartoryski, an old love.

Corinna tried to show her interest, but truly she was more aware of the man beside her than of any of the bright luminaries pointed out to her. How could he talk so calmly, when her own blood was racing through her veins?

She said sharply to her dreaming self, He is simply being civil to a fellow English person, one who will be connected with him one day. The silent reprimand did no good.

She had not the slightest doubt that he was a willing party to the arrangement the duchess had announced to them. Surely even that evil old woman would not try to marry Almira to a man who was less than willing. Besides, Justin was not one—so thought Corinna—to do anything he did not want to do.

Almira was so beautiful—so young and fresh. Justin might someday wish that she were more intelligent, better educated, but one could not have everything, could one?

No, she repeated to herself, while Justin sat with her on a settee, near a window allowing a refreshingly cool draft of air to reach her, he was simply being civil to Almira's stepsister. In all likelihood, he had forgotten that kiss which had rocked her, forgotten it altogether.

She stole a glance at him from under lowered eyelids. He seemed oddly abstracted. Perhaps he did remember what had happened on the packet. Perhaps he even feared she would tell Almira about it. Well, she would put his mind at rest on that subject, tell him it meant nothing to her. But not quite yet. A little longer she would sit beside him, tinglingly aware of the masculine scent of his tobacco and his shaving soap, and listen to his pleasant voice pointing out to her the various notables who passed in gala finery before them.

Justin spoke knowledgeably about the celebrities who shone brightly in the Viennese night skies, but only a small part of his mind was engaged in doing so. A much larger share of his thoughts wrapped themselves around Corinna, sitting demurely beside him. He had thought he could offer for her at some convenient time in the future when she, and he, and the mood together were favorable. But he had been occupied elsewhere, by Castlereagh for one, and he had missed her. God, how he had missed her!

And he had determined that he was going to offer for her the first moment he could. That moment was now. He turned to her, and found that his tongue was unaccustomedly thick, and the words would not come.

Corinna felt him shift his position. Now was the time! This tête-à-tête had gone on too long. The duchess would ring a peal over her, and rightly. She would tell him he had nothing to worry about from her—and then, lips opened to tell him, she had second thoughts.

Suppose he had forgotten it entirely? Then she would reveal herself to be a vulnerable, gullible spinster. She could not do it.

"Corinna—" he said in an altered tone. "I should like to tell you—"

The decision was taken out of her hands. Always considerate, unusually thoughtful for her as he had shown himself in the last weeks, he was now going to inform her of his approaching marriage to Almira, before such news came to her from someone else. She could not bear to hear him say the words.

She forestalled him. She turned to him and said gently, "Pray do not worry. You have been excessively kind to me." She could not meet his eyes. In truth her thoughts had played her false and become incoherent. Stumbling in her mind, she stumbled in her words. "Kindness is all you owe me—indeed, it is all I could wish for—"

"Kindness!" he blurted. "Is that all you feel?"

"Of course not. I must ever be grateful to you for your care of us all the way to Paris—and of course, for rescuing me from that horrid man—"

A small silence fell between them. Her mouth was dry and her thoughts riotous. What must he think of her? Suddenly, the realization swept over her that it would make no difference ever what he thought of her. She knew that after he married Almira she must go her own way. She could *not* bear to see them together!

For the first time in a long and well-favored life, Justin was nonplussed. The interview had taken a turn that he had not expected. He was chagrined, and disappointed. He could think of nothing useful to say. This fact did not prevent him from speaking.

"I fear perhaps you do not understand my situation."

Corinna, not experienced enough to retrieve the exchange with even the appearance of civility, nor even sophisticated enough to recognize that the gentleman had lost his usual address through sheer sincerity, plunged deeper into the pit she had dug for herself.

·"Believe me, Lord Lonsdale, I do not misunderstand you in the least. I cannot—I dare not—" At this point Corinna's evil genius surfaced and took charge. Drawing on her dignity, she told him, gently but with firmness, "I will not see you again, Lord Lonsdale."

"Justin," he murmured.

She needed to reassure him on the subject of that forbidden embrace on the packet. "I believe that in not much more than a fortnight I shall quite forget—everything—about you."

It was a blow. She had turned away from him, not daring to meet the expression in his deep blue eyes, so she did not see the color draining from his face. After days of brooding, he had talked himself into believing she returned his regard. In truth, he had hoped that she would leap into his arms, as she had, once.

He tasted ashes on his tongue.

"Then," he said thickly, "if you can abide the thought of remaining in my company for a few more moments, I shall escort you back to the duchess."

He helped her to her feet. His hand was cold on hers, and she felt sobs trembling in her throat. In frigid silence, not entirely unremarked by certain of those present, including the Princesse de Courland, and from an entirely different point of view, Lord Castlereagh, they walked together to the wide settee where the duchess waited.

The duchess drew Corinna down to sit beside her on the small sofa. "You stayed with Justin far too long. Everybody was watching you. I don't know whether I have credit enough to carry off such a scandal or not."

"Scandal?" said Corinna abruptly, nerves already

exacerbated. "We simply sat, at a ball, in full view of the company. No one could make a scandal of that!"

"What did you talk about?"

Corinna heard a note of suspicion in the duchess's voice, and managed to say, airily, "He was most enlightening. He told me who all these entrancing people are."

The duchess snorted. "I didn't like the way he looked when he brought you back. You didn't say anything to put him off Almira?"

"Her name was not mentioned." She did not think it was at all necessary to inform the duchess that while her name was not spoken, her existence was central to their minds.

"I'll not brook any objection to that match, Miss Darley. You may feel you have something to say to it, but you don't. Not a word. I am the only relative the child has, and I know what's best for her. Now fetch Hannah for me."

It would take longer than a fortnight to forget Justin, she knew. However, it must be done, and she had sufficient strength of mind to do it. But when they returned to England, she would not travel with Almira to Morland Hall. What should she do in England? She must put her mind to the problem.

But in the meantime, the present problem was, without the hope of seeing Justin, what would she do here in Vienna?

CHAPTER 15

The morning after the ball, Justin rose wearily from a bed in which he had sought sleep for long hours in vain. He had not known how much he had centered his life and his hopes around Corinna.

Nor, to do him justice, did he realize that he had committed the cardinal sin of one who would a-wooing go. He had begun to take Corinna for granted.

Not that he was so puffed up that he thought she would swoon at his feet—at least, not quite. It would be hard to say whether his understanding of her restricted life and her vanishing opportunities for marriage had influenced him, but certainly no suitors were visible on the horizons surrounding Morland Hall. He did not consider Mr. Willoughby. In reality, if that name had been mentioned, Justin would have been hard put to identify the man.

He did not try to analyze at first just what had happened. He was angry, hurt, bewildered. He had hoped, indeed more than hoped, and his hopes had been dashed in an instant.

The faintest lessening of the darkness outside his window told him that dawn was approaching, a new day of clouds, perhaps spitting snow, and a great emptiness in him.

Giving up any hope of sleep, he threw back the feather-filled quilts and reached for his heavy dress-

ing gown. He lit the bedside candle to dispel the
darkness of his thoughts. It did not help.

Standing at the window, hugging the wool-lined
brocade garment to him, he stared unseeing at the
empty street below. Even the tradespeople must
have found sleep this night, for no one stirred, not
the purveyors of victuals, the grooms, the emperor's
messengers.

Surely he had not been mistaken. She had a *tendre*
for him, he could have sworn so. His thoughts clustered around the feel of her. The wondering expression in her speaking eyes when she had fallen
almost into his arms, at the start—his anguish when
he had carried her, heavy as a dead body, into the
parlor at the Ship. And, again and again, her sweet
response to his kiss in the midst of a gale and storm,
flung spray and heaving deck. For that moment at
least, she had been entirely his. No thought of impropriety on her part ever crossed his mind. If
fault there was, it was his for rushing her.

He heard a tap on the door, followed at once by
the entrance of Francis, hair tousled, yawning.

"Just getting home, Justin?" he inquired. "A gala
night, I suppose?"

Justin turned, and Francis saw his expression.
"What happened?" he demanded, on a dismayed
note. "Don't tell me Boney's loose."

"Not that I know of. A bad night. I could not
sleep."

Grimsby arrived at that opportune moment—for
Francis, at least—with a pot of coffee and two cups,
and Justin was allowed a respite from his agonized
thoughts.

However, since there was nothing in the world
that was more important to him, he returned to
thoughts of Corinna. The interruption by Francis
had not blunted his misery, but it had allowed

other mitigating memories to demand his notice. He had been rejected, true. But, recalling every word of that conversation, held in full view of hundreds of guests in the Kaunitz Palace ballroom, he could not remember that he had mentioned marriage. Indeed, he had not!

But there was no denying that she had rejected him—I shall forget you in a fortnight!—even before he offered. Kind thoughtfulness, to save him embarrassment? Perhaps.

He smiled grimly. She had known what was in his mind, that was evident to him. And therefore it followed—it must follow—that they were in a sympathy to a degree.

The street below, as he finished his cup of cooling coffee, was coming alive, with horse-drawn carts, small carriages, and many people on foot. The assemblage of the leaders of four countries had drawn petitioners, gamblers, all the riffraff from all of Europe, seeking to pick up crumbs from the negotiating table, or, if possible, to prey on their fellows. Futile, greedy, distasteful—

When Francis spoke suddenly, Justin started. "I thought you had gone."

"I wish I had not had to leave you in Dover. But I was promised here in Vienna as soon as possible. Did you see much of Miss Morland on the journey?"

Justin was not tactful. "Enough. After we crossed the Channel and arrived at Paris, you know I was required to consult with the duke, and he kept me a day too long. I arranged for the ladies to join a much larger party setting out for Paris. I thought it best not to travel with them, under the circumstances."

"Very wise." Francis nodded knowledgeably. "With such a beautiful woman, one cannot be too casual about the proprieties." He took a deep breath, and added, "She is so beautiful!"

"Yes, she is," agreed Justin. "Perhaps her features are not out of the ordinary, but her hazel eyes are wonderful."

"Hazel?" Francis was indignant. "They are blue as can be."

Justin stared at him. "I collect," he said presently, "that you are not speaking of Miss Darley?"

"No, no. Surely you must admit that Miss Morland is a beauty? How you must have enjoyed her company those weeks in Kent. I wish I had not stayed in Vienna. I should have gone with you to fetch her."

"I saw very little of Miss Morland. Or Miss Darley, for that matter. I had affairs to deal with at Plowden Hall, you remember. There was much to be done."

Francis nodded wisely. "But she is lovely, and such an amiable disposition—" He stopped short when he saw the sudden gleam in Justin's eye.

"Amiable? She is like quicksilver, going in whatever direction is easiest at the moment." He did not continue, but he could have told Francis about the girl's selfishness, her wayward temper, which caused Corinna to appear more and more weary. He had hoped to see Corinna happier in Vienna—even hoped to be the cause of that happiness—but now he would be fortunate to catch a glimpse of her across a room filled with strangers.

But Francis, intent on his own thoughts, ignored Justin's comment. "I wonder why Cousin Maria has brought her to Vienna. To bring her out into society? I had not expected such generosity from our cousin."

"It does not sound like Cousin Maria," Justin agreed, "to do any kind deed without hope of reward. Probably she expects to marry the girl well."

"She is far too young for marriage!" protested Francis. "At least, not too young, but certainly too green."

"Perhaps not marriage," said Justin, without putting his mind to the conversation. "The duchess may wish Almira to seduce someone in the French delegation so she can get the Carignac lands."

"Seduce?" Francis echoed in a quavering voice.

Justin glanced swiftly at his young cousin. It was clear that Francis had developed more than a passing interest in Miss Morland. Quickly, to ease Francis's mind, he added, "Cousin Maria is daft if she thinks Talleyrand will move on the end of her string."

"Does she have a match in mind for Almira?"

"God knows. I don't." Watching Francis through narrowed lids, Justin thought it wise to give a word of advice. "I suggest you not go overboard in your pursuit of the girl."

"Overboard?" Francis added something that sounded like "too late."

"Don't throw yourself at the child's feet. You will not wish to raise her expectations, unwittingly, of course. She is very young, and her character is not fully formed." It was as gentle a warning as he could manage.

Suddenly sober, Francis answered, "I know that. That is why I think it is important to have things settled between us as soon as possible. The girl has no experience, and is prone to swing around like a weathercock, persuaded by the last person who talks to her. What she needs is a steadying influence. Someone she trusts enough to obey."

"Like an affianced husband?"

"Just so. I know I could see that she came to no harm while she gained a little polish. I do think she has some regard for me, but Cousin Maria's eyes shoot daggers when I call on her." Francis paused, then asked diffidently, "Do you think you might speak on my behalf to Miss Darley? She has great influence over Almira. A word from you—"

A log snapped in the fireplace and threw up a bright flame. Francis saw Justin's expression fully, and caught his breath, stunned.

Harshly, Justin said, "A word from me to Corinna would successfully dispose of any hope you might have of making progress with that schoolroom miss."

Francis stared. The beginning of an idea about the cause of Justin's sleepless night, of his hitherto unaccountably indifferent responses to Francis's praise of Almira, crept into his mind. Justin was blue-deviled, and it was up to Francis, who owed him so much beyond his deep affection, to come to his aid.

Justin of habit was used to keeping his private thoughts and wishes precisely where they should be—locked in his own head. But to his surprise he heard himself saying, "I've lost everything."

Francis had never heard that note in Justin's voice. He had not been made privy to Justin's hopes, but he was not blind, and even a witless fool could see that Corinna had dealt him a leveler.

Justin continued, almost as though talking to himself, "Can you encompass the thought of a lady of restricted means, sufficient to provide a modest living, comfortable but no more, turning down a future of leisure, of indulgence in travel, in books, of being mistress of her own household?"

"She didn't!"

"Apparently," said Justin savagely, "the thought that I was part and parcel of the future offered to her was sufficient to make it unacceptable."

"Justin! You must be mistaken!"

Justin turned fiercely on him. "You think I cannot understand 'no' when I hear it?"

There was nothing useful to say. Fortunately Francis was not obliged to give further comfort, for he had none to give. Somewhere Justin had put a foot wrong, and perhaps the match could be salvaged. But this moment was not the time to suggest any remedy, for he would have to start with Justin's own fumbling mistakes. Already, Francis had a strong suspicion of what had gone wrong.

"Not Miss Darley? She's gone witless if she refuses your offer." Francis wished he had bitten his tongue off before speaking in such derogatory fashion about Corinna. But apparently Justin had not heard.

Justin believed Corinna was clearly a woman to know her own mind. His own fortnight on his estates, going over the accounts, renewing his acquaintance with his tenants, had settled his mind on one thing. His days of derring-do, of dangerous deeds and perilous forays, were in the past.

From now on all he wanted was to sit by his own fireside, to have his own spaniels yelping around him as he walked to the stables, to hear his great stallion whinny a welcome at his approach—and to share his life with Corinna. How would he go on without her? Where had he gone wrong, so that she had taken such a strong dislike to him?

He did not realize he had spoken aloud until Francis answered him. "What a hum! Anyone can see that Miss Darley is swooning for you!"

"I cannot believe that. She told me outright—" But even to Francis, Justin could not reveal that his darling Corinna was so far from being enamored of him that she could forget him in a fortnight.

"I never thought the day would come, Justin, when I could instruct you. You do not see the glances sent your way when you are in company. I swear I hope she is discreet. The czar might have you kidnapped and sent to Siberian exile if he suspects she has a *tendre* for you."

"She told me I was kind—and she was grateful!" The words rasped like sand on stones.

"I remember," reminisced Francis, apparently at a tangent, "José Mirales spinning you the most probable yarn, with documents, proofs, all the facts in his hand. And yet he couldn't fool you for a moment. You knew at once that he was lying. Now comes a straightforward lady, intelligent, articulate, and she tells you the wildest Banbury tale imaginable, and you believe every word."

Justin was as a man revived from drowning. Perhaps there was hope after all. "Suppose," Justin began, "you wished to recommend yourself to—let us say, a lady. How would you set about it?"

Francis at last had attained a dream. His magnificent, knowledgeable, wise cousin was asking his advice. *His*, Francis's!

He had advice and to spare in storage.

"I never thought the day would come when I could instruct you." Honesty stopped his tongue. "I have not done well enough myself to serve as a prime example!"

Belatedly, Justin remembered a word from Francis's remarks. "What about the czar?"

"Obvious," pointed out Francis, somewhat giddy from his newly recognized authority. "He's after Miss Darley."

"No!"

Francis looked at him quizzically. "I swear, in your state of mind, I hope Boney stays where he is. If you take the field against him, scouting him out, you won't make it through the first day. You've lost your wits."

"Not my wits."

"Your eyesight, then."

Justin put his hand on Francis's shoulder in a kindly fashion. "Thank you. Don't worry. I'll take it from here."

Corinna must not be allowed to flee from Justin into the arms of the Russian. If Alexander was indeed stalking his Corinna—Justin noted with wry amusement that he had gone from desperation to optimism in a well-spent and full hour, to speak of *his* Corinna!—he would answer to Justin, czar or not.

CHAPTER 16

Justin was not the only person in Vienna troubled in mind. Corinna was quite plainly in the mopes. She had come to Vienna with vague but pleasant-hued dreams, and while she had held firmly to the tenet that she expected nothing from Justin, no matter how close they had been both at Morland Hall and on the first leg of the journey, she knew that she had been mistaken.

First there had been his abrupt withdrawal from her company. He might well have spoken truth when he explained the need for Miss Morland's party to join a larger company to traverse the uncertain roads through Germany. But there had been no reason she could discern for him not to accompany them on the longest and most tedious portion of the trip.

The final blow, the death knell, the end to the hopes she had not previously recognized, had come from the duchess. "Almira will marry Lord Lonsdale—it is all arranged!"

And while he was betrothed to Almira, he had paid particular attention—very particular!—to Corinna. Indignation provided a remedy for unhappiness, at least occasionally. How dared he treat her so? Did he think she might become a convenient supplement to his marriage?

Corinna was not overly experienced in the ways

of the world, but her few weeks in London previously provided her with food for thought now.

At any rate, she decided, remembering her interview with him last night, she could find satisfaction in having forestalled him in whatever he was
about to say to her. She had thought at the time
that his intention was to tell her, at last, of his
betrothal to Almira. Now the long dark hours of the
night had revealed monsters that she had not seen
before. She wondered whether he had been about
to suggest that she might have no objection to their
continuing their pleasant relationship no matter
what his future marital situation might be.

She pounded her fist into the pillow in sheer
outrage, and found that it was wet. The tears began
to flow in earnest then, and she fell asleep before
they stopped.

In the morning, Emma as usual brought two cups
of chocolate into her bedroom and settled for a
chat.

"How lovely you looked last night!" said Emma.
"I saw that a very distinguished person let his eyes
linger on you for more than a little while."

"Yes," said Corinna, holding a tight rein on herself, "we spoke for a short while. But I was merely
being civil, you know."

"I did not see that encounter. But of course you
must be civil to him. Only, my dear, remember his
reputation! He could be no more than flirtatious,
and I must beg you not to refine too much on his
attentions."

Emma's advice ran in quite startling parallel to
her own darkest suspicions. However, Corinna was
no more constant in her affections than Almira, for
at once she sprang to Justin's defense. "I did not
know of his reputation. And I wonder, Emma, why
you did not mention your doubts when he first
came to Morland Hall?"

"Morland Hall! When was the czar at Morland Hall, pray tell me?"

"The czar! Good God, Emma, you were not speaking of *him*?"

"Who else?" After a moment of recall, she added in a different voice, "Oh, Lord Lonsdale. I did see you returning to the duchess, and I would wager that he was not best pleased."

"Nor," Corinna pointed out, "was I."

They were interrupted by the entrance of Almira, dressed in the furs that the duchess had provided, and wrapped to her chin in a voluminous fur-lined cloak. Aunt Maria at least had the appearance of generosity, Corinna thought, but remembered Emma's suspicion that the furs were only lent, not purchased.

"Where are you off to today?" asked Emma. "Shall I go this time?"

Almira's glance moved uneasily from one to the other. "Oh, no, dear Emma. I shall be well taken care of."

"By whom?" insisted Emma. "After all, Corinna and I are charged with the responsibility for you."

"Yes," said Almira in a dry tone, "although the duchess says—no matter. However, today I am going with Lady Norton—her husband is on Lord Castlereagh's staff, you know. I am not quite sure of our destination, but you see you need not worry."

With a sunny smile, she was gone. Emma considered resuming her cautionary discussion with Corinna, but the ripe moment was gone, and soon she too departed.

Corinna cared little about how she spent the days, and did not stir herself to go into society. She dismissed Emma's claim that the czar had turned an interested eye on her—sheer rubbish. He had so many gorgeous, sophisticated women falling at his feet, besides his lovely blond Czarina Elizabeth.

If she had not known the difficulties of getting back to London, especially during the winter, she might easily have abandoned Almira to the tender care of the duchess and Emma and set forth on a homeward journey.

Certainly Emma was taking good care of Almira, for she was gone from morning till night. She had apparently decided not to leave her own duty in the hands of Lady Norton in every instance.

Corinna was too occupied with her own low, dismal thoughts to pay much heed to anyone else. Nor did anyone care greatly about her, she believed. Almira could ruin herself, Emma could elope with Prince Talleyrand, and the duchess could stuff herself with comfits till she died of them—and none of this would affect Corinna, for their lives went on at some distance from her.

A pleasant thought, she told herself. If I matter to nobody, then they do not matter to me, and all the burdens I carried during the year since Sir Rupert died and all was thrust on me—all the uncertainty and the hurtful rejection by Almira—none of this is mine anymore.

And if, as Emma had hinted, the czar himself had more than a passing interest in her, Corinna was free to dally—or not, as she chose.

But suddenly, a tap at the door brought her up short, and tumbled her out of her mopes. For one fantastic moment, she thought, Who stands outside? The Czar himself—his bright eyes, his thin lips, his hair arranged to hide his incipient baldness, his fresh complexion preserved by, so it was said, washing it every morning with a piece of ice?

She smothered her amusement at her own fancies when, upon invitation, Nellie entered.

Corinna stared at the girl. "Are you not supposed to be with Miss Almira?" she demanded. "Has something happened to her?"

"No'm," mumbled Nellie, looking at the floor.

"Where is she then?"

"That's just it, ma'am, I don't know."

Corinna sat up straight. "What do you mean, Nellie?" she asked in a monitory voice.

"It is what we both mean, Miss Darley," said a gentleman standing behind Nellie, whom Corinna had not seen until that moment. A fine figure of a man was Francis Ferrington, she thought absently, a thoughtful man, a considerate and intelligent man—and not a patch on his cousin Justin. Then his presence aroused her gravest suspicions.

"Mr. Ferrington! Now I collect something is sadly amiss. Tell me at once," she begged. "What has happened to Almira?"

Worried though he was, and he was anxious indeed as well as obscurely frightened, Francis saw no reason to omit the niceties of civilized behavior.

"I must apologize for troubling you at this early hour, Miss Darley."

"Early?" she echoed. "It is past noon."

"And that must be my excuse, ma'am, for Almira— Miss Morland, that is—is engaged to me for luncheon. She failed to meet me in the blue salon here in Kaunitz, as we had arranged—"

Corinna caught her breath with surprise. "But she is with you! She told me so not two hours since. You were to take her sleighing—I can see I surprise you, sir."

"We had no arrangement to go sleighing, ma'am, today or any time soon. And if you will forgive me, the weather is most unsuitable for outdoor amusement."

He glanced toward the window, and Corinna followed his look. She saw dark gray skies, clouds boiling with wind, and she heard the sound of needlelike sleet rapping on the pane. No weather, she had to agree, for a sleighing expedition. She should have noticed. And so should Almira, who should learn, if she was going to pursue this kind of life, to be more plausible when concoting her lies, For lies, Corinna suspected with sinking heart, were what were facing her at this moment.

"I should have realized that you certainly would not take her out in such a gusty storm. And you have been in each other's pocket so much recently—although I cannot approve under the circumstances, yet I feel sure she will come to no harm with you, Mr. Ferrington."

He nodded slightly, acknowledging the compliment. "But I beg your pardon, ma'am," he protested. "In each other's pocket? I do not think seeing Miss Morland not above once a week quite qualifies for that sort of intimacy."

"You cannot be serious! Once a week? Fiddle! You take her out every day."

Realizing that Nellie was an avid if somewhat apprehensive witness of this discussion, Corinna was about to dismiss her and then thought better of it.

"Nellie, where have you and Miss Almira gone this past week?"

"Nowhere, ma'am."

Corinna's brows drew together. "You cannot mean you do not intend to tell me where you have gone, Nellie."

"No, ma'am. I mean, yes, ma'am, I'll tell. Somebody ought to know. But I haven't."

"Come, Nellie," said Corinna in a pleasant but very firm voice. She was well acquainted with Nellie. The maid was sorely distressed, and Corinna knew she should have made inquiries before. But what was there to make inquiries about? Even yet, she did not know. Nellie held at least one key to the problem. "Start at the beginning, and we will come soon to the end." She glanced up at Francis, whose thin dark face was sober.

"Ma'am, it's not what you think. I would tell you in a second, so I would, did I know. But Miss has gone off alone. Not alone, either, but—" Nellie twisted her skirt anxiously.

Corinna summoned patience. "What you mean, Nellie, is that Miss Almira has gone on her outings and not taken you along?" Nellie nodded. "And who went with her?"

"I dunno."

"Was it Foster, the groom?" Corinna probed gently, as though testing a sore tooth. "Or Tyson, the coachman?"

Nellie continued to shake her head. "It's no use, ma'am. I dunno who went with her." The maid's indignation had been slowly rising for some time. At the start she had regarded traveling to foreign lands as an outrageous turn of events, and she had been justified by the results.

Sick as a horse she had been on the water coming across, and rightly, since it was against nature to set foot on water. As you might say. And now young Miss gallivanting off wherever it might be, with not so much as a maid to keep her company and fend off the villains that abounded everywhere away from Morland Hall. Look at what happened to Miss Corinna there, and they not yet out of England at the time! It was not what she, Nellie, was used to.

"Then she must have met someone at some place away from the palace. Nellie, you don't know—?"

"No, ma'am." And if Nellie had any suspicions, she was not about to air them. Corinna knew she would get no more information from this source.

"Very well, Nellie. You ought to have told me before, you know."

Francis waited until Nellie had closed the door behind her. "Do I understand correctly, Miss Darley? Miss Morland has been gone every day for at least a week without even a maid to lend her countenance?"

Corinna was irritated. "Of course you understand correctly. As I do. But pray do not pull a long face with me, sir, for as you gathered, I was under the impression that you were her escort. And, of course, I would have expected you to insist that Nellie go along."

"As, of course, I would have. But as we have learned, your impression was incorrect."

Corinna put out a hand to silence Francis. She had the feeling that he was wielding a hammer, and raining blow after blow on her defenseless head. First Almira's idiotic behavior going out without even the semblance of a chaperon, and then revealing to her the extent of the girl's gross deceit.

In her agitation, Corinna rose, and set to pacing the floor. The sitting room was hardly large enough for more than six steps either way, insufficient to relieve her feelings.

"Do you mean," she burst out, "that you have not been with her even once when she told me she was with you?" An involved sentence, she knew, but he caught her meaning without difficulty.

"I think perhaps we should compare notes, Miss Darley. I have not seen her this sennight, except at the balls."

"And did she not say anything—any hint as to where she had been?"

"Not a word."

Corinna grew more and more anxious. She must know what Almira was up to, and she dreaded beyond anything to find out.

"But where was Emma? Where was the duchess?" She stopped and looked directly at Francis. "Pray do not think I am handing off my duty, but in truth Miss Sanford was particularly charged with Almira's affairs. Under the duchess's instructions, of course."

"Emma Sanford?" Francis, whose private reflections told him there was no time to lose in bringing lovely Almira under his own steadying influence, took opportunity to assuage his curiosity regarding Miss Darley, his cousin Justin's nemesis. He had paid little heed to her before, being stunned at the start by Almira's fresh and incomparable beauty.

Now he saw that Corinna was enormously attractive. Not her features, perhaps, but he was struck by the animation that drove her, the flashing anger in her great eyes, the quickness with which she got to the heart of the matter.

"If you mean Miss Sanford," he repeated, "then I take leave to tell you that she has leaped over the traces with a vengeance."

"Don't be vulgar," said Corinna automatically, and then spoiled the effect. "What do you mean, leaped over the traces?"

"Miss Sanford is generally regarded in Vienna as a spy."

"Surely not!"

"Whether for Castlereagh or for, say, the King of Prussia the gossips have not quite determined."

She put her fingers up to massage her throbbing temples. "Truly, Mr. Ferrington, it seems to me you are speaking gibberish! Nellie must be mistaken. Surely Emma has been with Almira on every occasion! I see you do not think so. Perhaps you are right. But you know the duchess has instructed me not to meddle in Almira's affairs."

This was true, although she had never told anyone. The injunction had come during a private interview initiated by the duchess, who told Corinna without shillyshallying—"I pride myself on plain speaking," said the duchess—that Almira was *her* affair, and above all Corinna must not make sheep eyes at Lord Lonsdale. Corinna, stung, had taken such fustian as simply an attempt to wound her, and did not take it seriously.

"I fear you are mistaken in Miss Sanford's whereabouts," said Francis gently. "She slips privately into Prince Talleyrand's rooms in late evening, I am obliged to tell you. And what her purpose is no one knows. Although," he added, "to be fair I must say that so many explanations are offered that it is likely none of them is correct."

"You tell me nothing I don't know, Mr. Ferrington, for Emma has told me. She has a passion for music, and that is all."

"I must assume the rumors are false then."

"I am totally distracted! I must require Emma—no, that is wrong. She is not responsible to me now. But why is she not with Almira in the day? Mr. Ferrington, I must ask you to believe me when I say that you are stirring up a mare's nest. I know Emma well. She may leave Almira alone, in the late evenings when the girl is in bed. But I will not admit that Emma has allowed her to go out on the town alone."

"The maid did not mention her," said Francis quietly.

"No more she did. But I warrant you, Emma is with Almira at this moment!"

It was too bad that the second tap on the door in an hour gave the lie to Corinna. She might have been fortunate enough to escape this interview with Mr. Ferrington with the assurance that all was, speaking as to decorum, in good hands.

But chance was against her.

Emma followed directly upon the knock at the door. She was mildly surprised to recognize Mr. Ferrington, but her business was with Corinna.

"My dear, have you seen Almira? She was to meet me here this morning, and I quite forgot the time. And now I cannot find her anywhere in the palace."

A muttered and probably profane word escaped Francis's lips, and, although Corinna did not hear it precisely, she shared its heartfelt quality.

"She was to meet you here?" asked Corinna, and at the same time Francis exclaimed, "But she was to be with me at luncheon!"

The three looked at each other in mounting wonder and, in the case of one at least, a wish to take the child by the shoulders and shake her till her bonnet fell off.

"I see," said Mr. Ferrington stiffly, "that you ladies will wish to have private converse over this, and I will take my leave. In the meantime, perhaps I may catch sight of her—somewhere."

Somewhere, let us hope, within Vienna! thought Corinna, only half jestingly.

After he had gone, Emma, finding that her knees were unreliable, sank into a chair. "I cannot believe— you surely do not mean that that wretched child— but, Corinna, where did you leave her this morning?"

"Surely you realize by now that my dear stepsister has diddled us all? She told me she was to be with Mr. Ferrington. She told you, if I understand you, that she was going out with me." She waited for Emma's impatient nod before she continued. "And that is not the worst of it. She left Nellie at home, and—dear God!" Corinna put her hands to her face. "She has been playing us for the fools we are for weeks!"

Stoutly, Emma protested. "It is my fault entirely. You could not be expected to disbelieve her."

"I cannot think why not. We have had a fine example of her dependability before we ever left Morland Hall. Imagine her writing to the duchess asking for a dowry, when she had sufficient of her own!"

"That was Jack Hardie's doing, I make no doubt of that. But that is nothing to the purpose now."

"What is to the purpose," said Corinna fiercely, "is what I shall say to her when she returns!"

"Should you not go to the Duchess?"

"She would leap to blame you for the business, my dear Emma, and I refuse to sacrifice you when it is Almira's doing."

"I should hate to leave Vienna," sighed Emma, "especially now, when—"

Now was the time for Corinna to inquire about Emma's late-blooming interest in Talleyrand's pianist, but she was prevented. The door burst open and Almira came dancing into the room. She had apparently just come from outside, for her cheeks were rosy with cold, and the fur of her collar was wet with snow.

"Oh!" she said, clearly dismayed. "You're both here."

"Of course we are," said Corinna with deceptive mildness. "Did you enjoy your morning?"

Almira eyed them warily. "Yes," she said shortly.

"And did you meet Mr. Ferrington for lunch?"

"N-no, Corinna. He didn't—did he come looking for me?"

"You really must take better care of your scheduling of engagements," Corinna recommended. "Events are so prone to overlap, and then, dear Almira, the fat is in the fire."

Almira realized then that she had been found

out. And while she did not feel that she had done anything truly horrid, yet she knew the value placed on more conventional behavior. Also, she had learned that denials carried little weight unless she managed to assist them with a display of temper to cloud the issue. She proceeded to do so.

"I've done nothing! You're the ones who are ruining everything—you're spying all the time!"

"Spying!" cried Corinna.

At the same moment, Emma said sharply, "Almira!"

Corinna accused, "You've been meeting someone clandestinely in the most commonplace way—and I can only hope he is a gentleman. Without a maid, without your chaperon! What will happen when the duchess hears about this?"

"You won't tell her?"

"You can be sure that Hannah will hear of it, and I should not be surprised to learn that the duchess already knows. We may expect to be sent home at once."

"Do you think she would? I would like that above all things! J—" She faltered and then continued, "Just that I am tired of Vienna."

Corinna, while newly realizing that she did not understand Almira as thoroughly as she had thought, nonetheless believed that the child was about to say something else. "J—." Could she have been going to say "Justin"? And had her escapades been mounted with the sole purpose of being alone with her unofficially affianced husband?

At the picture suddenly conjured up in her mind, Corinna was revolted. Justin—and Almira!

Corinna tasted ashes on her tongue.

CHAPTER 17

Corinna, no matter what Francis had said, or even considering Almira's offhand confession, did not wish to believe that Justin would be party to a plot to deceive Emma, or anyone else, for that matter.

If Justin had beguiled Almira into traveling about Vienna with him alone, without Nellie or Emma, then she, Corinna, would never trust her own judgment about a gentleman again.

It was time to consider her own situation. She was here in Vienna almost against her will and certainly against the duchess's wishes, expressed in no uncertain terms. Corinna had thought that perhaps Justin's company might be sufficient reason to stay—but how mistaken she had been!

Now, of course, winter had set in—it was already January, and from all reports Vienna was locked in, and few travelers came across the long leagues from France. The only travelers who arrived in the city were messengers carrying dispatches, and those she could almost wish might be snowbound in some chalet in the Alps, for Mr. Willoughby's letters came in great volume, if not containing much of compelling interest.

The only good thing about the severe weather, she thought, was that Mr. Willoughby was still in London, and not, as he had suggested more than once, on his way to her side.

Corinna was not in charity with anyone she knew. She was certainly not in the pocket of Almira. That young lady was currently under the blind, uncertain guidance of the duchess.

Nor was Emma in the least sympathetic. Emma had fallen into the same trap that she had wished for Corinna—a few weeks and a world away, chatting idly over morning coffee. Emma was head over heels infatuated with Talleyrand's musician, Neukomm. Perhaps not with the man, but certainly Emma was enthralled with the liquid notes that came from the piano late at night, soothing Talleyrand, and filling the soul of Emma, sitting hidden in an adjoining room. She soaked up music as though she were a dry sponge. Corinna had not realized how deprived Emma must have been, in the dull life at Morland Hall.

But most of all, Corinna realized to her sorrow, Justin had no true interest in her. She had, after all, continued to see him at least in company with Almira and Emma, and had even shared a sleigh with him on rides through the snowy streets of the capital, tucked into a sledge shaped like a swan or a tiger, covered with fur blankets, with Justin handling the reins as the vehicle flew over the packed snow—and those rides had been marvelous. Even knowing that the second sledge, driven by Francis and carrying Almira and Emma, followed directly behind them had not spoiled the sense of being alone with Justin.

When she was honest with herself, she had no doubt that Justin arranged these excursions to gain Almira's favor—as the duchess had pointed out—and only chance and Francis's deft maneuvering put Corinna cozily in Justin's sledge, and kept Almira and of course Emma in his own.

During these days, Corinna more and more often

sought company with Dorothée, Princesse de Courland. The elegant woman of the world held fascination for Corinna. While Dorothée's conversation sparkled like a malicious girandole—if one could imagine such a prodigy—she was entertaining in the extreme. Her gossip was current, and her outlook was pragmatic and cynical.

Corinna had been brought up carefully, and the idea that the loss of her virtue, or even the appearance of having lost it, meant for all practical use losing the rest of her life to degradation and social isolation had been drummed incessantly into her ears.

Both the shame and the solitude she had now—the duchess lost no opportunity to berate and sneer at her, and her friend Emma and her stepsister were intent on their own diversions.

And in all this, Justin could not help her. She had told him she would put him out of her mind in a fortnight. She was wrong. He persisted, like a burr caught in a woolen skirt. She had tried to whip herself into an indignant state of mind over him, telling herself that he intended to marry Almira and keep Corinna attached to him, but it was no use. She could not see him in such a role, no matter how she tried.

Well—there was only one thing to do. She must fill her hours in Vienna with other things, leaving no time for regrets.

It was at this crucial juncture that his majesty the Czar of All the Russians was at loose ends, and admired her again at a dinner in the Upper Belvedere Palace.

The first intimation Corinna had of Alexander's interest, sincere but certain to be fleeting, was when a bouquet of roses came to her. The deep crimson velvet of the petals brightened the small sitting room, and she turned to Dorothée, who had entered on the heels of the messenger, and said, "Thank you so much! These are just what I need, for my spirits have been declining all day."

"Don't thank me," said Dorothée, amused. "I did not send them."

"Then who?"

"I have a good idea. But is there not a card?"

Corinna probed gently at the bouquet. "There is something—let me get at it." In a moment, her fingers closed on something hard and cold. She pulled out a slim handful of green and gold and glittering white.

"Mon Dieu," exclaimed Dorothée. "Why would he send emeralds? Surely he has noticed you do not wear green."

"They are not real, of course," Corinna said, but at base she had the strongest impression that the flawless emeralds and diamonds set in gold were as genuine as the Crown Jewels in the Tower. The bracelet was heavy in her hand, and surely their purity could not be matched by strass, or paste.

"Of course they are!" Her friend laughed. "Make the most of it, while you can. If you go at this in the right way, you may make your fortune in a fortnight."

Corinna stared at Dorothée. "You know who sent this?"

"Of course. Alexander did. His majesty is prone to these little gestures. You will next have an invitation to open a ball with him, and who knows what happens after that?"

"But why me?"

"But why *not* you? You are exceptionally attractive, you know."

"I don't know any such thing," said Corinna, irritated by the unwanted gift, and more than a little suspicious that she was dipping her toe into deeper waters than she knew.

"You think only of that vacant beauty of Miss Morland's. I tell you she could not hold the interest of any man above the level of idiot for more than half an hour."

"Mr. Ferrington seems quite taken with her."

"I think not for long. He will see that she comes to no harm with him. But I should be much in error if he weds her. Already I see in his eyes the *ennui*."

Dorothée regarded her friend, speculation in the dark violet eyes. Should she inform Corinna of the dangerous game the young fool was playing? Or should she allow the girl to get into such trouble as she would? Dorothée, not caring much for more than a handful of the people around her, dismissed Almira without regret. Corinna deserved better than a stepsister who traveled with questionable young Englishmen, without chaperon and, thought Dorothée, without any sense whatever. She would not trouble Corinna with trifles.

"What shall I do?" said Corinna.

"Wear the bracelet tonight. Alexander will know what next to do. He will make all arrangements. Don't ask me arrangements for what, *chérie*. He simply admires pretty women, and thinks they are placed in life for his enjoyment."

"Then I have nothing really to fear from him?"

"I cannot promise you, but I believe that rarely does he pursue any lady to the ultimate."

Corinna suddenly laughed. "How shocked Mr. Willoughby would be at our conversation! He would come no matter what the weather, if he heard!"

"By the time he got here," Dorothée pointed out calmly, "your little *affaire* would be done with. And you would have enough jewels to cushion the rest of your life. And I shall hope that that life will be

spent not with that peasant who writes you those
volumes—Mr. Willoughby!"

"Be assured it will not!" Corinna added, troubled, "I cannot use his majesty thus."

"But he is using you, you know."

In any event, the bracelet went back to his majesty at the Hofburg Palace, with a pretty little note
thanking him for the roses, and not mentioning the
unacceptable addition to the bouquet.

She would not have been human, however, had
she not felt a certain satisfaction in the knowledge
that she had had wealth in her hand and an illus-
trious admirer at least figuratively at her feet. And
she went with Dorothée to a magnificent ball given
by the Russian ambassador in honor of his sovereigns.

Justin, following his discussion with Francis, had
taken to heart some of the advice given by the
younger man. Justin had never preened himself on
his address with females. He had not the ways of
flirtation, being essentially a serious-minded gentleman. He had thought he recognized a sympathetic person in Corinna, and her recent behavior
had left him all at sea.

But if Francis was correct, then perhaps all was
not lost. If he had misunderstood Corinna, then
there was hope for him, provided he mended his
ways with her and studied to improve.

He had moved too swiftly, he decided. His ad-
vances to her had met with gentle rebuff, but perhaps her refusal to see him except in company was
simply her way of suggesting that he behave more
circumspectly. He was desperate to believe there
was hope for him.

While trying to decide just how to take the first
step toward getting himself into her good graces, he

dropped into the Russian ambassador's ball. And there was Corinna, on the czar's arm, stepping out in the majestic opening movements of the traditional polonaise.

Francis was at his shoulder. "I told you the czar was taking an interest. Look at the way he leans over her, as though not to miss her slightest word. God, he's a vain man."

"Quiet!" whispered Justin fiercely. "You want to get us thrown out or more likely knifed on the way home? Besides, it's only because he's deaf in that ear."

He had thought that Corinna was not indifferent to him. He was apparently mistaken, but—he valued Corinna. And he could not be content to see her as an adornment, no matter how temporary, at Alexander's side. He did not know how long he stood there, listening to idle comments around him—"Who is the English lady with Alexander? Not his type, I should have said. This one—plain as dishwater. But she does know how to dress." If Justin had known, Dorothee's tutelage was apparent in that last remark.

The opening polonaise was over, and the dancers moved at random across the ballroom floor. Justin caught sight of the lovely blond Czarina and her Prince, apparently indifferent to the throng, but Elizabeth's eyes followed her husband. Her gaze was intense, and Justin curiously followed its direction.

The Czar, Corinna on his arm, was moving toward one of the anterooms that lined the ballroom.

"Surely, your Majesty—" Corinna objected.

"Why are you fearful, my dove?" The Czar spoke excellent but heavily accented French. "Merely a small glass of refreshment, does that not charm you?" Anticipating the withdrawal from his forearm of her small hand, he covered it with his free hand and pressed her fingers intimately. "Ah yes, you are very warm."

Actually, she was icy pale and shivering with cold, as Justin, standing nearby, could see.

Justin threw his carefully thought out plan for wooing Corinna—starting at the bottom and moving with circumspection and purpose through the varied steps of courtship—to the winds. The Czar was not to be allowed even to caress Corinna in the slightest degree—to say nothing of whatever else he had in mind.

With deceptive casualness Justin moved swiftly to intercept them. He had had some experience— perhaps not with women, but with enemies. As though by chance, he stood blocking the door to the withdrawing room that seemed to be the object of the Czar's progress.

According to protocol, the higher-ranking gentleman must speak first. The Czar, unused to persons who stood in his way without moving, stared down his nose at the interloper. Justin merely smiled and waited.

Corinna could have died of embarassment. There would be a scene. Everyone in central Europe was watching, and at this moment she could have killed Justin. Cheerfully.

At last the Czar, seeing the only other way to resolve the situation must be to push the man aside, chose to speak. After all, one never knew how these mad Englishmen would react.

"Ah, Lord—is it Lonsdale? I find it difficult to recall your English names."

This, thought Corinna, on the verge of unseemly giggles, from a man who can rattle off names like Michael Ilarionovich Kutuzov and Fedor Vasilievich Rostopchin without a second's hesitation!

"Your majesty," said Justin formally in French, the language of diplomacy, "I regret excessively, sir, that I must beg a word with Miss Darley."

"No!" said Corinna, but not aloud.

The Czar merely lifted an eyebrow, a gesture calculated to wither the intrusive Lord Lonsdale where he stood. Justin appeared not to notice.

"I have word for her from her grandmother in London," he said brazenly.

Corinna gasped, amazed. What a bouncer!

"Such word, I collect, must be in the nature of an emergency?"

"Quite so, your majesty."

"And cannot wait?"

"Precisely, your majesty."

"Very well." He gently removed Corinna's hand from his forearm, kissed her fingers, and smiled ruefully down at her. In some ways a realist, he noticed that the flush on Miss Darley's cheeks was vastly becoming, but he was well aware that it was not caused by his own proximity to her nor his well-known charm.

"My dear," he said, "if Bonaparte had been as clever as you, and possessed such support from his friends, we would not yet be discussing peace."

He bowed over her hand, and, ignoring Justin, turned and left them alone together.

Corinna, though greatly relieved at Justin's intervention, nevertheless thought it impolitic to express her gratitude. She was forgetting him, was she not? And even a simple thank-you might lead to who knew what.

"I have no grandmother, Lord Lonsdale."

"A pity. You must have had one once." Corinna's apparent anger evoked an unfortunate response from him. "But obviously not. No grandmother would bring up a granddaughter to allow the Czar to take liberties—"

"Take liberties! You are insulting! I have allowed no liberties from him or anyone else!"

Suddenly each was visited by an identical memory—a treacherous deck beneath their feet, strong arms wrapping around her, sweet lips uplifted to his—

"At least—" she began, and stopped. With an effort, she whipped up her indignation again. "Why I should feel obligated to explain my actions to you, I cannot tell!"

"I have your interests—"

"Pray do not bam me! Why should you have my interests at heart? When I return to England—and frankly, I pray God that will be soon—I shall go my own way, and it would be surprising if our paths crossed again."

Justin, a man of iron self-control when faced with peril, did not recognize the present situation as one of danger. He was bewildered, at a loss. And he lost his temper. It was not apparent to an onlooker, of whom there were several evidencing fascinated interest, that he was filled with rage. "Shall I return you then to the duchess?"

With a lift of her chin, she said, "Since you have completely ruined my evening, you may take me back to the Kaunitz Palace. Pray make my excuses to Almira."

"Almira," he echoed, startled. "What has she to do with anything?"

"How greatly you sound like your cousin Maria," said Corinna with a sweet smile. "I must tell you, I do not consider it a recommendation!"

They waited in silence while a footman retrieved wraps. When Justin was informed that his carriage waited, he touched Corinna's arm and guided her out of the Russian embassy by a side door.

The attendants were noticeable by their absence, he saw idly, all having gone inside to watch the dancing. His own men would know better than to deviate from his instructions by the least tittle. Apparently the Russians held to odd ways. But there was no danger in the short walk to the carriage, here in the embassy grounds.

A large leafless shrub marked a bend in the walk. As they came abreast of it, a dark shape loomed up, a man with heavy stick in his hand, upraised ready to descend.

Justin had no need to think. Automatically one hand went up to twist the assailant's stick-wielding arm, and the other moved skillfully to use the man's neckcloth to cut off his wind. The assailant in a trice was on his knees, clawing at his throat with his free hand and making ugly noises.

Corinna, moving so that the light coming from the distant windows of the building fell on their attacker, cried out, "What is he doing here? Justin, it's Jack Hardie!"

It was indeed Jack Hardie. And why he was there, lurking in the dark, hoping for a chance no matter how remote to put paid to Justin Ferrington, he could not have satisfactorily explained.

He had followed them from London, to abduct Almira and, although his plans were not detailed, to extract Almira's dowry from her aunt. Although dowry meant marriage, and he was not loath to wed Almira, the immediate need was not for a wife but for sufficient money to pay his enormous debts. He could not ask his father again to pull him out of the River Tick, for he had all but refused the last time. But at Dover, Jack had made another mistake.

The lady strolling outside the Ship was not Almira, but Corinna, and her rescuers were too soon on the scene for him to make himself known.

Now he was in Vienna, and his gambling luck was no better than in England. He had only that afternoon cast his dice for the last time—and not at the baize tables, either.

The Duchesse de Carignac had been surprised to see him.

"Has Almira not told you about me?" he asked smoothly.

"No, and I do not wish to hear. Tell me at once why you came to me, or I will have you thrown out."

"I think not," he said. "You will not wish to cause a scandal by evicting your niece's betrothed."

She sat stunned for a moment. "I will cause a scandal when I wish," she said defiantly, but her heart was not in it. "Tell me how this comes about."

Jack told her, spinning a tale about young love thwarted by evil enemies, a gentleman (himself) forced to make his expenses by gambling, his luck departing.

"Then," she said astutely, "you want money."

"How very clever of you," he said approvingly. "Not a loan, of course, for that would be tedious to repay. Especially since you and I are about to become related."

The duchess was furious. "Almira will marry Lord Lonsdale. It is all agreed. I would never allow her to marry a cheap gambler like you. Get out. Hannah! Come at once, and call the guards!"

Hannah appeared at the door. Jack hastened to forestall his eviction. "You think Almira will marry Lord Lonsdale? Not a chance! I wonder why you would entertain such a folly."

"Folly, is it?" said the duchess, moved to reply.

"I wish it, that is why. She will be settled for life. Lonsdale is very warm, you know, and he will not ask for much in the way of dowry. Why should he? He's rich as a nabob. And Almira is a beauty, you can't deny it."

"Now I understand," said Jack approvingly. "Set the girl up with no expense to yourself. I said we were two of a kind, both of us with an eye on the dibs."

"That is not it," said the duchess without conviction.

"Then, let me guess. You wish to tap into the Ferrington fortune yourself? Don't count on it. You will have Corinna to deal with first."

"Corinna?" screeched the duchess. "She has naught to do with it."

"Lonsdale is after her, don't think otherwise. Of course, I could give Corinna a whirl myself. Take her out of the picture, you might say."

"I don't understand."

"I daresay Corinna'd be grateful enough to see me. A face from home, you might say, and not Willoughby's, either. I'll need an advance on expenses, you know. If I'm to cut out Lonsdale, it'll take money."

"How much?" asked the duchess faintly.

"Ten thousand pounds." She gasped. "To start with," he added hastily.

"Impossible!" she shrieked.

"Now then, young man," said Hannah in her hoarse voice. "Best get out. Now."

He eyed the duchess warily. In truth, he would be glad enough to get out of there, for the woman's face was crimson, and a little thread of foam emerged from the corner of her mouth.

"All right," he said quickly. "I'll get out."

But, he added to himself, Lonsdale has got to be

dealt with, if he's supposed to marry Almira. The girl—and her dowry—are mine, by right!

In her own way, the duchess too realized that she must deal with a situation she had not been aware of before. If Justin was after Corinna, instead of her own Almira, then the situation must change.

She had not the slightest doubt that she could deal, very effectively indeed, with Corinna.

And Jack went into the night to deal effectively, so he thought, with the high and mighty Lord Lonsdale.

CHAPTER 18

So Jack Hardie had been an unseen member of their party all the way from Morland Hall!

Corinna had paid no heed to Jack's protestations that he had just arrived in Vienna and had not had time to seek them out, not knowing their precise direction.

It would be folly to think that Almira was not aware of Jack's nearby presence. How else was she to explain Almira's frequent absences, her lies about where she was going or where she had been? No wonder Justin was disgusted with her, Corinna. For if Corinna was expected to keep Almira in pristine innocence until her marriage with Lord Lonsdale, she had signally failed.

Emma came in then, and, after looking gravely at Corinna, said with a casual air, "I heard there was some trouble last night at the Russian ambassador's ball."

"You are just the one I want to see," said Corinna cordially. "I have so much to tell you."

"I fancy I have heard the most of it. You and Lord Lonsdale attacked by some lout with a grudge against him? Did you learn who he was?"

"I had no need to learn, Emma. Nor would you. A grudge perhaps, but more likely against me. It was Jack Hardie."

Emma sat down abruptly. "Then he's the one."

"What do you mean?" demanded Corinna.

"The duchess has been complaining—"

"She usually does."

"She says that Almira is not fulfilling her duty. She doesn't make herself available when Justin calls, and she seems actually to avoid him."

"Then," said Corinna in a flat voice, "he does call. Even, I suppose, fretting because Almira is not at hand. I wish him well," she added in a voice manifestly insincere.

Emma cast a shrewd glance in her direction. She knew very well which way the wind blew for Corinna, and she had seen not the slightest evidence that Lord Lonsdale had even a passing interest in Almira. No man of sense would!

"Corinna, you're foolish. Lord Lonsdale formerly came here—and I admit he calls no more—only to see you. I suspect you have said something to turn him away."

"I told him," said Corinna hollowly, eyes on the leaping flames in the fireplace, "that I could forget him in a fortnight." She heard a sound from Emma that could be described as a snort, but she knew it well as a symptom of disapproval. "Well, what else was I to do, Emma? I could not encourage him— even supposing he were to pay me attentions—when he is promised to Almira."

"Fustian! He does not give me the impression of a man whose interest is fixed, at least on her."

"And I did think he was interested in me, for you know he is quite the most sympathetic person, but I thought he simply had it in mind to be nice to his affianced bride's stepsister."

"Corinna! I quite despair of your good sense. No man is going to go out of his way to charm a mere connection."

"Perhaps not. But Emma, I have refused to see

him, I have quarreled with him—the reason we came upon Jack was that Justin was escorting me to his carriage to bring me back here."

"Out of sight of the Czar, out of mind? Don't goggle at me, Corinna. You did not think you could forever hide all those little nosegays? You dealt very properly with those gaudy jewels he sent you."

"Oh, Emma, and you said nothing!"

"What was there to say? I have eyes in my head, and I can certainly see that Lord Lonsdale would offer for you in a minute, given half a chance. And you must whistle him down the wind! I declare, Corinna, is it your *choice* to retire to a small house in Bath?"

"No," she said in a small voice. "But the duchess said—"

"The duchess," said Emma stoutly, "has no affinity for the truth." They heard a step in the outer room, and turned to the door. "Ah, there you are, Almira," Emma continued. "And how is Jack? His wrist hurts, I collect?"

"How did you know? That odious Lord Lonsdale was so cruel! There was no need for him to attack Jack!"

"You are mistaken," said Corinna firmly. "It was Jack who sprang out of the bushes and would have felled Lord Lonsdale if he had been able." She raised her hand. "Do not tell me otherwise, Almira, for I was there and saw the entire incident."

"Oh!" Almira sank limply into a chair and covered her face with her hands. We will be fortunate if we are spared a screaming tantrum, Emma thought. But Almira had been severely chastened in the last weeks, and she said now, in a muffled voice, "Aunt is after me again to marry Lord Lonsdale, and I cannot."

"How is this?" wondered Corinna. "Has he spoken to you?"

"I have not even seen him—except, of course, in company—for a month. You know he and Mr. Ferrington used to take us riding in those darling swan sledges? But that was long ago."

"All of a month," murmured Emma dryly.

"Let me understand this," insisted Corinna with a deep need to ferret the truth about Lord Lonsdale's marriage plans. "You and Justin have not spoken of marriage?"

"How could I when I'm promised to Jack?"

"How promised?" demanded Emma, darkly suspicious.

"We are going to marry, when we have enough money. And Aunt Maria won't give us any. Jack told me to tell her that she could save all the money on bringing me out, and giving me a fashionable wedding, and just give me the same amount."

Emma thought it quite likely that Almira would see little enough of the duchess's money, either on wedding or entertainment, unless she could bring Lord Lonsdale up to the mark. That, Emma told herself, remembering the determined jaw and the sharp intelligence in him, was as unlikely as she herself marrying Talleyrand. Or Neukomm, she added, sadly. The musician or the music—she could not determine which she loved, but she knew she would be desolate without either.

"And I'm sorry, Corinna, I never thought he would hit *you*."

"What?"

"That night in Dover. I was supposed to meet him, and I did say I had the headache and I went upstairs, but I could not get away, for there were too many people on the stairs, and so he made a mistake."

"A mistake," repeated Corinna ironically. "But what matter, it was only my own head, and it is not the only mistake he has made."

But whatever more she might have said to Almira went unsaid, for Hannah came with a summons to the duchess's presence for Miss Darley.

"She is yours, Emma," said Corinna, gesturing toward her stepsister, now bent over in her chair, the very picture of despair. She herself followed the gaunt figure of Hannah out of the room.

Corinna realized within moments of entering the duchess's small sitting room that this was to be no ordinary interview.

The duchess was crimson wth rage, as blood-red as the ruby necklace at the edge of the table beside her, and Corinna suspected that it was not a sudden anger newly come upon her. Remembering all Almira's deceit, and her refusal to give even the appearance of trying to attract Lord Lonsdale, Corinna had a glimmer of the causes behind the duchess's rage. She must have arranged a marriage to suit herself, but surely Justin must have known what his cousin planned. There was much to be explained here. She might, in some future time, ask Justin. The thought betrayed her.

"Don't smile at me, young woman!" cried the duchess. "There is nothing in the least amusing, let me tell you! When I am through with you, you will wish you had never come to Vienna."

Corinna gathered her thoughts. The duchess was gravely disturbed, and Corinna must step carefully. "I already wish so, ma'am, on my own account. But I do not understand you."

"A young lady without scruples, I see. Perhaps you will inform me, Miss Darley, how it is that you could so deliberately bring shame upon my head?"

"Shame?" echoed Corinna, bewildered. "Surely—you cannot think that I allowed his majesty to take liberties with me?"

For a moment, the duchess was taken aback. "His majesty? No majesty has aught to do with anything! A parcel of posturing fools, the lot of them!"

Corinna realized that the scarlet-faced duchess must be in a fair way of suffering a seizure. She deliberately spoke in an even tone. "Then I don't understand you."

"You came here without being invited. I should have suspected you then! Out to thwart me at every turn. Well, young lady, I've had enough."

"I fear," said Corinna, watching the duchess gulp several times before speaking again, "that I must leave you. You seem quite ill. Shall I call Hannah?"

"Ill! I guess I am! To think of you and that young Hardie fellow, a loose screw if ever there was—"

"Me? And Jack Hardie? Oh no, you are mistaken, ma'am."

"Am I? Do you deny that you and that man connived to foil my plans?"

"Yes, I deny it."

"It takes more than a mincing miss to outwit me."

The woman was in desperate earnest, thought Corinna. She must do her best to calm her down. She was talking the most outrageous nonsense—but there must be some kernel of truth at the bottom.

"I should not dream of attempting to circumvent you," she soothed. "But perhaps if you were to make all clear to me, I could explain."

The duchess became calmer. Miss Darley was behaving in a surprisingly innocent fashion. It might be that she was mistaken in the smaller, insignificant details. But she had no doubt at all that Miss Darley was guilty of the main charge.

"All right. I have no proof that you and that fellow connived to get him here."

"The last thing I would do, ma'am," said Corinna, encouraged by the duchess's approach to reasonableness, "would be to arrange anything with Jack Hardie. I find him crude and vulgar, and not entirely to be trusted. I must tell you, however, that his family is next neighbor to Morland Hall, and he and my stepsister are old friends."

"She'll not marry him." It was a dogmatic statement.

Corinna was not entirely sure that Almira had not already wed Jack, in a secret ceremony. At any rate, Corinna would not care to attest to Almira's spinster status, to say nothing of her virginity.

"I suppose the young man would not like to see Almira's acres pass into the hands of someone by far his better," the duchess speculated.

"The acres, ma'am, are numerous, but not greatly productive. Nor are the buildings in good repair. It would take much to put them into condition, I am told, and I cannot see Mr. Hardie taking the trouble."

"Nor do I. But my nephew could well do it, and you have done everything you could to thwart my plans for their marriage!" Aunt Maria's voice was rising again. "My niece will wed Lord Lonsdale! No matter what obstacles you put in my way."

Should she suggest to the duchess that Almira might not be free to wed? That would surely bring on the threatened stroke, and Corinna bit her tongue on the words. "I collect you think I planned to bring Jack to Vienna? That I have been a party to Almira's continued and unexplained absences? If anyone has planned to thwart the marriage you planned, I think you must look to Almira and Lord Lonsdale themselves. I have nothing to do with it."

"Do you deny that you have been in Justin's pocket ever since you arrived?"

"I certainly do. I have not seen him except in company for weeks. Believe me, I have not tried to thwart your plan. In truth, I have deliberately sought other entertainment. Pray think again, ma'am, for how could I arrange with Jack Hardie to foil your plan when I did not know it when we left England? Not until we arrived here—"

"Uninvited, you were!"

"Very well, uninvited. However, you must know that Almira would not have come without me. But as I said, you must look more closely at your plans and at the intended happy couple to find the defect that balks you. It is not I."

There was a long, long minute when the duchess, breathing heavily, glared at her out of small eyes nearly hidden by folds of flesh.

"Then, suppose I believe you. Will you promise me to return to England at the first opportunity?"

"I shall be happy to return," she said evasively.

"And not speak or write to Justin, ever again?"

"Now why should I promise you that? I have told you that I have rebuffed him—"

She had made a mistake. She felt as she imagined one must feel who had stepped thrustingly onto a tussock of grass in the middle of a quagmire, and found it sinking beneath her.

"Rebuffed him! Then you *are* trying to inveigle your way into his fortune! I was right at the first!" Her voice rose to a shriek.

Corinna, equally angry but with more control, sprang to her feet. "How dare you!"

Hannah had entered the room, silently as always. Now she spoke in her rusty, unused voice. "Best leave, miss, or you'll kill her!"

Corinna whirled on the maid, indignant denials

on her lips, but she did not speak them. She was insensibly moved by the naked concern in the servant's eyes. "Yes," she said, suddenly deflated. "Yes, I will go."

"Out of Vienna, you'll go!" screeched the duchess. "Out of my rooms in an hour, or I'll get the guard to put you out in the street!"

Corinna bowed. "I shall leave as soon as I have packed," she said, hardly knowing what she agreed to.

But when the duchess fired her final salvo— "And promise me to stay away from Justin!" —she knew how to answer. "I owe you nothing, ma'am, and I will promise you nothing. Besides, what Lord Lonsdale does is not in my control!"

CHAPTER 19

Corinna did not remember traversing the short distance to the rooms she shared with Almira and Emma. She hurried through the reception room, dropping her reticule on a side table and seeking refuge in her small sitting room beyond.

She had long since given up expecting any service from Nellie, who was after all Almira's maid, and she longed in vain for a cup of hot, restorative tea.

How dared that aunt of Almira's accuse her of such odious behavior? Never in her life would she have set out deliberately to entice a man from his affianced bride. Not even Justin—although the thought gave her an unpleasant pang.

Corinna sat in one of the chairs drawn up to the hearth, and knew she was excessively weary. But the urgent representations of her thoughts could not be dealt with unless she stood.

And, of course, once standing, she began to pace back and forth. "To think," she said aloud, "that I have come all this way to Vienna, to lend Almira the countenance she needs, simply to be insulted."

Right and left, she had been affronted. Upon her arrival the duchess had told her she was unwelcome. Emma had found a new, absorbing interest in her musician, and Almira went abroad every day and the truth was not in her.

Even Justin—Lord Lonsdale, she corrected herself, since they were no longer on easy terms—even he had thought fit to condemn her behavior with her dancing partner. Of course, the Czar did have a kind of reputation, and if she herself had seen Almira on his arm en route to a private anteroom, she would have had a hysterical fit on the spot. But Jus—that is, Lord Lonsdale, had no business to interfere. She was nothing to him.

The nub of the problem—she meant nothing to him, and if she was to be devastatingly honest with herself, he meant everything to her.

But to be told she was setting traps for him—outside of enough! "And where I shall go now, I haven't the remotest idea!" She did not realize she had spoken aloud until she was answered.

"My dear, are you planning to leave? I fear there are storms coming, and we shall be snowbound in Vienna until March at the latest. Already it is January—"

Emma broke off when she caught sight of Corinna's ravaged face. Corinna had been left alone quite long enough, and while Emma did not understand Corinna's dilemma, at least she recognized her great need for sympathy.

"Come sit down, my dear, and tell me all about it," she said, with a caressing note in her voice that quite undid Corinna. The tears brimmed over and slid down her cheek, and, without comment, Emma handed her a clean handkerchief.

"You will not believe it," began Corinna, "no more than I did—"

After she had heard the story, Emma was thoughtful. "I cannot let you go home alone. You really believe she means to remove you by force?"

"She certainly said so," reflected Corinna, presented by Emma with the first suggestion of doubt.

"And I tell you, Emma, no matter how dreadful and unjust she is, I do not wish to be responsible for her death."

Emma started. "Corinna, pray do not do anything you will regret."

Her misunderstanding did much to restore Corinna's poise. "You did not think I would take a pistol to her? Where would I find one, in the first place? No, no—you did not see the woman's face. She was already crimson when I first went in to her, and she finished with a complexion turned an interesting shade of magenta. I know I am babbling, Emma, but I am trying not to think—I consider myself fortunate to have left her before she had an apoplexy."

"Yes, of course," said Emma, a trifle absently. "But you think she will not reconsider? Do you expect truly to be forced to leave?"

"Yes, I do." Suddenly serious, she wailed, "Where can I go? Snow is thick on the ground, and the passes doubtless cannot be traversed. And—look, Emma, more snow is starting to fall."

"Whatever you plan to do, Corinna," said Emma stoutly, "I will go with you."

"Emma! You are a darling, but you must not! I will hire a maid here and we will go—perhaps to Italy. I have not been there. We will go on the stage—I am sure they must have stages here?" While Corinna's words, and the tone in which they were uttered, seemed lighthearted, even a touch frivolous, Emma was not deceived. She saw the haunting fear behind the hazel eyes, and felt some of the same desperation gnawing at her.

It was difficult enough to be English in a foreign capital if one had sufficient money to buy whatever services might be obtainable, at enormously inflated prices. Corinna was in funds, but without a protector, without influence, one simply did not go out and hire a carriage and a coachman and two footmen and a maid—the barest minimum of escort to be considered.

"But I cannot let you go alone—"

They had not heard Hannah come into the sitting room until she spoke. "Go, miss? Nobody is to go."

See? said Emma's glance at Corinna. The duchess didn't mean what she said.

"Her grace is sending for the guard."

"Guard? I expect to have sufficient time allowed to pack and make a decent departure from the Kaunitz, from Vienna, and I shall make all possible speed," said Corinna with dignity.

"No, miss," argued Hannah. "You're to stay till she finds the necklace."

"Necklace?" echoed Emma.

Corinna looked more closely at Hannah. She thought the old servant might not agree entirely with her mistress. Certainly Hannah, while appearing as vinegary as usual, had altered, in a way Corinna could not precisely analyze. But there was no point in thinking about Hannah herself. What dealt Corinna a blow was the message she had brought. With an effort, Corinna probed further.

"Now, Hannah, you had best tell me about the necklace."

"Yes, miss. The ruby one with the diamonds. Worth I dunno how much. A mort of money, I can tell you that. And it's gone."

"Stolen?" interposed Emma. "When did your mistress see it last?"

Hannah's eyes moved restlessly. "I got 'em all out this morning as always. Her grace says tell young miss she's to wait and be arrested."

"For what?" demanded Corinna. "I have not seen that ugly necklace, nor would I ever wear such a vulgar jewel."

Hannah stared at the floor. "Worth a mort of money," she repeated. "Her grace is past the prime of her life. Best wait for the guards."

"You may tell your mistress—" began Corinna on an ominous note, but Emma interrupted.

"Hannah, you may go." After Hannah had left, Emma pointed out, "The woman was simply following her orders, Corinna. You have no quarrel with her."

Corinna's fists clenched. "I will not wait to be searched by any guard, I may tell you at once." Then, in an entirely different voice, she moaned, "That horrible necklace! Oh, Emma, what am I to do?"

"I confess I am at sixes and sevens, my dear, but I think I know what we shall do first. I think we both need a cup of tea."

Two cups of tea apiece later, there was still no clear-cut plan to follow. Emma was determined that Corinna must not be allowed to depart Vienna alone. "I should not sleep a wink, thinking of all the perils on the road. Only last week I learned of a convoy of six carriages buried in an avalanche."

"But I should not go into the mountains, Emma."

"There is no way out of this place that does not involve mountains. Perhaps not the highest, but certainly even the valleys in the direction of Italy must contain avalanches, or impassable drifts, or highwaymen. No, I won't hear of it."

"But you cannot desert Almira!"

"She does not need me. In truth, I rarely see her. But Nellie sometimes goes with her. I do not envy the wench, waiting in anterooms while her mistress does—who knows what?"

"Had you thought," continued Corinna, determined that Emma must not sacrifice herself, "that the moment the duchess learns that you are with me, she will send word off to her friends in London? It could be that she will lie in such a way as to preclude your ever getting another position, and while I would be delighted to have you live with me, I do think you must not burn your bridges."

In spite of her sympathies, Emma could see that Corinna's argument was valid. And she could not expect Corinna to support her for the rest of her life.

They sat in silence for a while, each wrapped in her own thoughts, which, while they ran along different lines, were equally gloomy.

Then at last Emma stood up. "I must talk to Sigismund. He may think of something."

After she left, Corinna's thoughts were all at sea. Sigismund? Oh, yes, Talleyrand's musician. Apparently Emma had progressed in her acquaintances beyond the rapt listening in an anteroom while he played for his master. *Sigismund* sounded like a very close relationship.

And Corinna had made so little use of her time in Vienna that she had no one who could help her. Justin was the only one whom she might have turned to, in other times, but no more. She could not ask him even for advice. And besides, his aunt would be even more furious if Corinna approached the man she had marked for Almira.

In addition, that ridiculous accusation about the necklace put all at hazard. She had not taken it, of course. She thought she could remember seeing it on the table beside the duchess just before she stormed out. She had no fear that the guards could find any tangible evidence on which to arrest her.

But she had no intention of undergoing such a degrading search. The palace guards might even now be on their way to her sitting room. She must leave—but she was not packed and had no place to go.

Suddenly the one person in Vienna who could help her came to her mind. "If you ever need me—"

If ever she did need the Princesse de Courland, it was at this very moment!

Time was running out. She must not be found here when the guards came. She paused only to snatch up a warm shawl that lay on a chair, and as she hurried out through the reception room she picked up her ample reticule from the table where she had dropped it. It seemed heavier than usual, but she had changed some bills, and doubtless it was the weight of the gold coins in change that caught her notice.

She hurried into the corridor. There was no one in sight. At least she had forestalled the guards. She ran down to the end of the corridor and looked out across the lobby of the palace. There were always people in the lobby, suitors trying to get favors from the prince. Even from here she could recognize the King of Denmark and three princes and dukes of small principalities whose lands had been overrun by Napoleon and who now wished them back as they had been before.

But no guards.

She tucked her shawl tightly around her and picked up her skirts. She moved swiftly, trying not to run and thus call attention to herself, through the throng and up the broad marble stairway at the far end of the lobby.

In a few moments she was hurrying down the corridor that led to the rooms of the princess. Just outside the white-and-gold door she paused. What could she say?

The outrageousness of her errand to the princess swept over her, and stopped her with her hand

upraised to knock. What call did she have to enlist
Dorothée's support? But she recalled her kindness
not only that first day, but in an occasional ten
minutes in a withdrawing room at one of the many
balls, or that advice Dorothée had given her on the
occasion of the emerald bracelet from the Czar.
Whether the errand was outrageous or not, the truth
was that Corinna had no place else in the world to
go. She tapped on the door.

The princess was not in.
The maid was adamant. The princess was not
in—at least she was not in to company. Could word
be sent to her? Of a certainty, *non, hélas non.*
Corinna had counted on Dorothée. How much,
she knew only by the trembling in her knees and
the pounding of her blood in her head when she
was disappointed.
Corinna groped for a nearby chair, and the maid—
Marie, that was her name—sprang to help. She
eased Corinna into the chair and stood looking down
at her.
"Some brandy, miss? I get it."
In a very short time, Corinna was sipping a brandy
of whose excellence she was scarcely aware. She
felt the warm tide of the restorative moving through
her body, and at once felt better, but her tears
continued to flow unabated.
"*Quel dommage*, miss," murmured Marie. "Is it a
great trouble?"
Corinna nodded. "I should not have come. I
hoped—but it is too much—"
Her incoherence, while it spoke of confusion rife
in her mind, had quite the opposite effect on
Dorothée's maid. Her instructions were, of course,
definite. While her highness was engaged with
visitors—particularly of the masculine variety—she

was not to be disturbed. However, Marie was a born and bred realist, and while men may come and go, one's friends are one's sisters under the skin.

She vanished from the room.

Once her tears had started to flow, she could not stop them. She dared not return to her rooms, for the guards would by now be waiting for her, without doubt. Nor could she make her way out through the lobby to—well, to anywhere. It was January, and Vienna was snow-covered. Corinna had only her thin shawl, and her reticule that she had dropped to the floor beside her.

It was quiet here in the newly painted salon reserved for Dorothée's exclusive use. Corinna had been told that when the prince arrived in late September, he had found the palace almost a ruin. Moths had eaten their way through draperies, chair cushions, even rugs. All had been replaced, and Corinna thought idly of the great waste in letting such a magnificent building fall into dust.

She closed her eyes to ease their burning. She heard the slightest of sounds, a swishing as of satin moving over wool carpet, and opened her eyes hastily.

"*Chère amie,* what can have happened?" Dorothée, wrapped in a plum-colored satin negligee, appearing to have been donned in haste, was looking down at her with concern in her dark eyes. "Marie said— well, no matter what Marie said. You must tell me."

Corinna was no fool. Abstracted as she was by her own troubles, she still had a fairly accurate notion of the activity that had been until moments ago occupying the princess. "I should not have bothered you."

Dorothée gave a Gallic shrug of the shoulders, a gesture that threatened to dislodge the satin robe, and said, "It is nothing. Has Lord Lonsdale—no, an offer from him would not bring such fountains of tears."

"It is the duchess."

"*Mon Dieu,* what has she done now?"

Corinna told her the major part—that she had been as good as evicted—"from quarters she does not own," murmured the princess—"and there is no place for me to go. I thought you might give me some advice."

The princess was silent so long that Corinna thought she must have given offense. She gathered her shawl and bent to pick up her reticule. "I should not have come. Pray forgive me."

Dorothée roused. "What are you thinking? I should have been angry had you gone to anyone else. I shall manage all. Wait just a little moment longer, my dear, and I shall be ready—" She looked down at her robe as though she had not seen it before. "Ah, yes, I must dress at once."

"But the guards—" Corinna began, but she spoke only to emptiness, for Dorothée had disappeared into an inner room. Corinna had forgotten to tell the whole of it, because the necklace—that absurd necklace—must simply have been misplaced by the duchess. She suspected that by now the vulgar jewels would have been found.

She did not know what would happen next. She was in Dorothée's hands, and she had no fears for the future.

CHAPTER 20

Dorothée's little moment lengthened into almost an hour, but when she returned, she was dressed as elegantly as though she were on her way to an afternoon of leisure and enjoyment.

Corinna hardly noticed what her friend was wearing. The moment Dorothée entered, Corinna sprang to her feet. "I was—" She discarded the word "afraid" in favor of another, less revealing. "I was becoming anxious."

"I have not forgotten you for a moment. Is that all you brought with you? That shawl? And that ridiculous huge reticule?"

"I think I did not mean to return to our rooms."

"And of course you will not. Come with me."

They started from the room. Corinna stopped on the threshold. "You don't expect me to go back to the duchess, do you?" She remembered that last horrid accusation flung at her as she ran from the room. "I did not tell you the whole—"

Dorothée held her arm. "No matter the whole. What we must do just now is—best left in my hands, *chérie* Wait a little moment."

Dorothée emerged into the corridor and looked both ways. No one was in sight. "Now, come. Pray keep yourself from running. You have committed no crime."

"You don't know—" murmured Corinna, but Dorothée did not hear.

They met no one on their journey down the hall from the door of Dorothée's sitting room. The corridor stretched an interminable length ahead of them. Corinna had not the slightest idea of where they were going. They moved in a direction opposite to the rooms of the duchess, and Corinna was at least so far content.

Surprisingly to Corinna, she seemed to have relinquished all concern for herself. She had hoped for help from Dorothée, her last desperate hope, and she was justified. Dorothée was in charge, and—blessedly—Corinna had only to follow directions.

Perhaps tomorrow, she would begin to take stock of her situation and whatever possibilities might come her way to extricate herself from this ugly situation. Just now, she knew dimly that she was on the verge of nervous collapse. She had never in her life been so tired.

"Where are we going?" she asked at one point, seeing nothing ahead of her at the end of the corridor but a solid wall.

"We're going to get you to a place where the duchess, blast her soul, cannot follow."

There were more questions Corinna wished to ask, but truly she was too tired even to think about them. They did not, as she anticipated wildly, walk through the wall. Dorothée stopped before a small unobtrusive door and opened it.

"Here we are. We will now mount up the stairs."

Dorothée led the way up a steep flight of stairs. The stairway was so narrow Corinna could place her palm flat upon the walls on either side. Her hand came away dirty. It had been a long time since these walls had been painted!

Two turnings and they came to the top of the

stairs. They must be somewhere close under the roof of the palace, judging from the distance they had climbed. Where on earth were they?

Another small door opened from the landing, and she followed Dorothée inside.

It was a revelation! She stood in the doorway of a sparsely furnished but spacious room. A bed stood in the far corner, two chairs drawn up to the hearth, a useful table beside it. And wonder of wonders—a fire burning brightly, although there was a lingering smell of smoke.

The figure putting more wood on the fire stood up when they came in. "Sorry, your highness," she apologized. "The chimney, it was with the birds' nest, I think. It is cleared out now."

Corinna could not speak for wonder. The princess—or at least her army of servants—had made good use of the hour she had made Corinna wait. The bed was narrow, but the featherbeds were fresh and smelled of heliotrope. A fur-lined cloak lay across the foot of the bed, and beside it was without doubt a supply of nightwear and underthings.

"I am sorry that there is no place to hang your clothes," said Dorothée. "But you realize that we have not had an abundance of time!"

"I cannot think how this must have looked an hour ago, for everything now looks so new."

"It was of a piece with the rest of the palace when we arrived," the princess said dryly. "Full of ugly moths and holes in the carpets. And the cobwebs. How I despise cobwebs!"

"I cannot thank you—"

"Then do not try. You will not be here for long. I shall see to that."

"But I did not tell you the whole of it."

Dorothée did not appear to hear her, but in moments Marie was sent to bring a tray of food, and the two were alone. Dorothée closed the door behind her maid. "Here is the key, Corinna," she said. "This locks the door at the bottom of the stairs. Apparently this room was the abode of some unfortunate relative of the grand duke who built this monstrous building. You will not be afraid here? But you will listen for Marie's knock? She will bring your meals, and whatever else you wish."

"You are so kind." Corinna started to sit down, but she remembered the moths.

"The chairs are clean. They came from my own sitting room. Now let us sit and you will tell me the whole of it, as you say. It is not that I wish to know your secrets, *chérie*. It is so I know how to help you."

Corinna was near tears from the happy shock of her altered circumstances. "Why are you—?"

"I told you once we could have been friends. Now, I think we are. All right, dear Corinna—the whole of it."

Corinna related the whole of it. Another time she might not have bared her secrets so freely, but she owed Dorothée much so far, and in all likelihood her debt would continue to grow.

She had told her that she and the duchess had quarreled, or rather that the duchess had quarreled. "For all I did was listen. The things she said were such a shock to me! She accused me of such extraordinary things! Like conspiring with Jack Hardie, of all people, like trying to set a trap for Jus—Lord Lonsdale."

Dorothée listened without surprise. She had less than contempt for the duchess. She had asked her uncle why he allowed the woman to stay in the suite of rooms he had given her at the start. "Simply so I know where she is," Talleyrand had replied. "As long as she thinks I may return her husband's estates to her, she will hold her viciousness to herself. But if I allow a break then she is one more enemy to deal with."

"You could not set a trap for any man," Dorothée told her friend, matter-of-factly. "More's the pity." She eyed Corinna speculatively. "There is more, is there not?"

"She wanted me to promise not to see Lord Lonsdale."

"You were not foolish enough to agree?"

"No. But what he does is his affair. I have nothing to do with him."

"And you have told him so, I make no doubt. Well, all comes clear to me."

"But that's not the whole. She accused me of stealing. She said I took that ruby necklace. And I didn't! I couldn't have taken it, for she was watching me."

"You mean that excessively vulgar ruby-and-diamond necklace that's always on top of that pile she keeps on her table?" Corinna nodded. "Then do not worry about it. Of course you did not take it." Dorothée smiled maliciously. "If need be, I shall tell her that if you wished jewels, you could have kept the Czar's spectacular offerings. That will send her into hysterics, if not an apoplexy. Well, we may live in hope. Here is Marie with your luncheon. Eat well."

"But what am I to do?"

"Leave all in my hands. I will extricate you from all this."

"And I cannot repay you."

"Marie, set the tray down. I will follow you in a moment. Miss Darley has the key, and you will knock—so—and she will know it is you at the door."

"Thank you, Marie," said Corinna sincerely.

"Now then, let me ask you one question. If I were in trouble, would you help me?"

"As far as was humanly possible."

"That is repayment enough. Friends of that sort are in short supply."

Dorothée reached the door before Corinna thought of one last favor. "Could you tell Emma where I am?"

"I shall send word to her that you are safe. But where you are? I think I shall keep that a secret for a little moment. You do not need to talk this situation to death with her, and we know she would want to come to you at once. If she can wrench herself away from my uncle's pianist!" Dorothée reflected for a moment. "You know, *ma chère,* I think I shall arrange that match. Your Emma and Neukomm! She must be saved from the duchess, and certainly the woman is not a success as a chaperon!"

"Not entirely her fault!" suggested Corinna.

"No? Perhaps you are right. But we will leave her young charge to the formidable aunt. Now, my dear, I have to think out my plan. But you will be comfortable here, I shall hope, while I scheme my schemes! Trust me—I speak ten honest words in ten!"

Giving Corinna a glimpse of the smile so rare that many of her contemporaries did not believe it existed, Dorothée slipped through the door. Corinna could hear her footsteps fading away down the stairs. She was alone, in a safe haven. She was furnished with warmth and food—the aroma from Marie's tray hinted at one of Carême's masterpieces—and she was in no danger from palace guards or from freezing to death in a dirty Viennese doorway. Considering the alternatives, she was grateful, and almost happy.

*   *   *

In another palace not far away, the temporary
home of the English delegation, a serious discussion was under way.

Justin lounged against the mantel, his deep blue
Ferrington eyes fixed upon a pair very like his own.
His expression, however. was grave, while Francis's held a glint of exasperation closely akin to
anger.

"And do you know the girl has been diddling
them this long time? She told them she was with
you, or with me, when all the time she was with
that—that—"

"His name is Jack Hardie," said Justin evenly, "and
whatever else you wish to call him is nothing to the
point. You feel the girl is too badly compromised?"

Francis flushed. "I should not stop at that. She is
just a green girl, doesn't know how to go on. If I
thought she was the right one for me, I would tell
Cousin Maria to take her dowry and use it to clean
those ugly diamonds of hers. And take the girl back
to England."

Justin thought for a moment. "And weather whatever storm might come up? I don't doubt you are
right. In truth, I thank you for a lesson for myself."

"Good God, don't tell me you're taking over the
girl?"

"Lackwit! Of course not. But direct action may
be the exactly right thing to do. In your scolding for
Almira, had you thought how cast down her stepsister must be to learn of her deceit? To find out
that your only relation has been thoroughly untrust-
worthy for some time must be the source of great
unhappiness."

"Then you will elope with Miss Darley and take
her back to England?"

Justin stood, arrested. His eyes were focused on

the far corner of the room, and Francis recognized the signs of deep cogitation.

"Yes," he said at last, an excited note in his voice. "That is exactly what I will do."

However, his plan was doomed, for the present, to failure, and he himself was within moments to enter into the worst period of his life. The first step came in the form of a note from Emma Sanford, addressed to Justin.

"Now, here's a hen-witted—why on earth should Miss Sanford write to me? She says—" He read the letter quickly, swore, and read it again. The letter did not improve on second reading. "I cannot believe this. Why would she—?"

Francis, was by now thoroughly alarmed, not only from the disjointed phrases his ordinarily serene cousin was letting drop, but also from the sudden tremor in the hand that held the missive.

"Justin—tell me!"

"She's gone!"

"Almira? Eloped with that—? She's not so harebrained as that!"

"Not Almira. Miss Darley. This Emma—" He handed the note to his cousin. "This Emma says that the duchess has sent her away."

"How could she?"

Grimly, Justin strode to the door. "That is not the question, Francis. Where is Corinna, and is she all right? Those are the proper questions."

"Where are you going?"

"To talk to the duchess. I hope I shall merely talk, for already my thoughts turn on throttling her."

Francis, essaying a glint of dark humor to soothe Justin, said, "I doubt you can find her neck, in all those folds of fat."

*　　*　　*

Justin, in the event, kept his temper quite admirably. In fact, the duchess was so misguided, thinking herself in control of the situation, as to mention her wish that Justin would offer for Almira. "For there is a good bit of acreage with her, Justin, and the Ferringtons have always had their eye on more land."

Justin rose abruptly. "All I want from you, Cousin Maria, is to know Miss Darley's whereabouts. After that you and your niece can take up residence in Bedlam for all I care."

"Miss Darley, is it? You surely can't wish to marry her! Although I should not object to a bit of dalliance on the side—after you marry her step-sister."

"You cannot have heard me right. Where is Miss Darley?"

"I don't know, and I don't care. She's a thief, you know. Stole my jewels right out from under my very eye."

"Corinna stole your jewelry? Bedlam's the very place for you. Corinna wouldn't touch your baubles."

"Ah, Justin, so high and mighty? She did indeed. She took my ruby necklace, worth a thousand pounds at least. I sent the palace guards after her, you know, but she'd already decamped. And if that is not a sign of a guilty conscience, then I don't know what is."

He longed to wipe that satisfied smirk from the duchess's face, preferably by unrestrained force, but instead, suddenly, he laughed with genuine amusement.

"You mean that great red-and-white monstrosity?"

"My rubies and my diamonds," she said with dignity. "Worth I cannot tell you how much. A common thief she is. If you marry the girl, let me tell you I will not receive her."

"Believe me, you will not be asked to do so."

"Then what was so amusing?"

"You, Cousin Maria. You know to a farthing how much that necklace is worth."

"I do?" said the duchess uneasily.

"And so do I."

He reached the door before she called him. "Don't forget what I could tell the world about Francis."

"Don't forget," he said gently, "what I shall be happy to tell the world about you."

He was gone. The duchess bit her lip. All her plans had gone awry, and she was suffering the pains of great disappointment. That interfering Darley girl had got away from her. But the necklace was still gone. She had not returned it, therefore she was still genuinely a thief in possession of stolen property. If not precisely stolen, at least it was missing. Perhaps there was hope yet.

But again, Justin was a formidable enemy, and she had no doubts whatever that his cool toleration of her was at an end. She could not think of words harsh enough to describe him. Instead, in a sudden impulse, she reached out and swept everything off the table onto the floor, and the Ferrington tiara and a half-full cup of chocolate and a dish of dragées and the rest of her bracelets and her rings spilled onto the carpet and scattered.

"Hannah!" she bawled. "Come and see what Lonsdale's done!"

CHAPTER 21

Justin, balked by the usages of civilization from giving the duchess her deserts, stormed out of the duchess's reception room into the corridor. With no very clear idea of where he should start in the vital search for Corinna, he found he had turned automatically and stood now before the door to the small set of rooms allocated to the visitors from England.

He had raised his hand to knock when the door swung away from him. The Princesse de Courland stood there, clearly ready to emerge.

"I beg your pardon, highness," he said perfunctorily, and then, seeing that Dorothée wore an odd, speculative expression and was making not the slightest effort to allow him entrance, he added, "I have matters to discuss with Miss Sanford. May I enter?"

The princess took a backward step. "Of course you may enter, Lord Lonsdale. But I shall tell you that it is of no use to discuss matters with Miss Sanford."

Inside the room, he closed the door behind him. Clearly the princess knew something of Corinna's disappearance. "Then Miss Darley has not returned?"

"No, my lord, she has not. Nor will she while I have breath in my body. She is safe, and I have come to tell Miss Sanford so. Corinna asked me to do so, or I would not have thought of reassuring her friend."

He eyed the princess, who stared back with great self-assurance. She knew something—and clearly she could be induced to tell him what he wanted— needed—to know. "You know where to reach her?"

She nodded. He did not quite know how to phrase his next question diplomatically. While he hesitated, he was conscious of her measuring glance on him. Before he could speak, she demanded, "Lord Lonsdale, I am not often mistaken, and I am convinced that you are greatly interested in Miss Darley. Will you tell me the scope of your interest?"

Unexpectedly, Justin laughed.

"You find me amusing?" The claws were still sheathed, but the threat of danger was evident.

"Not at all, highness. It is simply that I had not expected to declare my intentions so soon—"

"And to me. I can see that."

Simply, Justin said, "I love her, and I wish to marry her."

"But you have not told her so?"

"She has held me at arm's length this long time."

The strangeness of this interview struck him with force. Talleyrand's niece was a luminary of the first magnitude in Vienna, but he was barely acquainted with her. And yet here he was confiding to her emotions that he would have died rather than express even to Francis.

"Pity," said the princess. "For now is the time she needs good friends."

"I am sure she is most fortunate to be acquainted with you."

"You have come from the duchess? She convinced you of the truth of her accusations?"

"Not for a minute."

He had apparently passed some kind of test, for

the grave features of the princess relaxed. "Very well, Lord Lonsdale. We may talk freely here, and I should not like you to be seen calling on me in my rooms. Pray sit here beside me. I have an idea. . . ."

At that moment, Corinna poked up the fire in her attic room and pulled up a chair to feel the warmth of it. She had slept well, under the feather-filled quilts. For once she had not traveled over old roads in her mind—roads that led to unanswerable questions, such as "What shall I do when Justin marries her?" and "How can I bring Almira to a sense of her outrageous behavior when the duchess tells her I am not to be heard?"

Now, the cocoon of hard, unpleasant duty surrounding her had been broken, past mending, even had she wished to. But yet there was no freedom for her.

A time of waiting, a time for doing—life moved in great rhythms. Now she had to wait. She was in Dorothée's hands, and helpless to know what she must do.

Dorothée would not allow the guards to take her away, and she was safe. But she could not live till spring in this small room, comfortable though it was, and depend on Dorothée's servants to bring her meals.

At least, she was innocent of theft. She could certainly prove that—if the police ever gave her a chance. She had no notion of the workings of the police in this country, but she knew better than to put faith in them, for the duchess was a wealthy and influential woman. No ordinary citizen of England would have been invited to stay in Talleyrand's palace!

The thought of Dorothée's maid came back to her. She must give Maria a tip for her willingness to wait on her. She had a few sovereigns and other coins in her reticule—fortunately, it was large enough to hold all her necessities of the moment.

She picked it up from the table and opened it, shaking it upside down to dislodge any coins caught in the lining.

Her heart stopped, and she could not breathe.

· From the pouch came a stream of gold coins, a handkerchief, the small key to her jewel case—and a heap of red stones and white, fashioned in a necklace setting of gold! The stolen necklace!

Her knees gave way, and she fell into the chair. The duchess's necklace. In her own possession. She could not think straight—but one thing she knew. It was not a stolen necklace, at least by her. It was a *missing* necklace, and she had found it. And she would return it and all would be well.

A moment's reflection banished that course of action from her mind. The duchess would never forgive her—not for taking the necklace, of course, but for causing Justin to jilt Almira.

Jilt? The precise word, for the marriage had been arranged.

She must think. The necklace had been on the table; she remembered now that she had noticed it when she had first answered the duchess's summons yesterday morning—noticed it, and thought in passing that it was badly in need of cleaning.

Then if it was on the table then, how had it leaped from the heap into her reticule? It could not have caught on her sleeve, for she would have noticed it at once, as heavy as it was.

But if it was heavy, why had she not noticed that her reticule had taken on weight?

Slowly she drew near to the answer. She had recently drawn a modest amount of money, for veils and small purchases, and dropped the coins into the pouch. The coins accounted for the sudden heaviness. But she remembered—when she had run out of her rooms to seek refuge with Dorothée, and picked up the pouch from the table in the reception room, she had fleetingly been surprised at the weight in her hand.

And who had come into the room while she was within, telling Emma the horrid news? The only person she was sure of was Hannah.

She had the answer. The duchess had sent Hannah with the necklace to secrete it somewhere in Corinna's belongings, ready for a search of her things when the palace guards arrived.

Well, she had forestalled the duchess, so far. The guards could not find her, nor would they find anything compromising in her trunks. But there was still the ugly necklace to deal with.

Always prone to fancy, she thought that Dorothée might betray her, that she would hear the sounds of heavy booted feet on the stairs, the guards would search her with rude hands, and the bracelet would be brought forth in triumph, the great rubies looking like her life's blood spilled on the table.

Hurriedly she thrust the jewels back into her reticule, out of sight, and snapped the clasp shut.

She did not know how she passed the rest of the day. She looked long from the attic window over the roofs of Vienna, seeing the great fretted steeple of St. Stephen's, the snowflakes coming from the low gray clouds over the city. She saw none of this.

Marie came with a meal, and came later to take it away. She looked without favor at the untouched tray. "You must eat, miss. How can you go on without the food?"

"I am not hungry."

"If you will forgive me, miss, you are already thinner than yesterday. Worry does not keep one beautiful. There is no need for care, for her highness has plans in the making."

Listlessly, Corinna roused herself to respond. The maid was trying to be kind, and Corinna could not be rude to her.

"Plans? I cannot see any way out of this terrible predicament."

With great confidence, Marie said, "There must be a way, and my mistress will find it, do not doubt it. There is nothing she cannot do."

Corinna glanced at her surroundings, conjured up for her by a figurative wave of Dorothée's magic wand. "I believe you."

The maid poured wine into a glass on the tray. "Here, miss. Her highness will not like her hospitality refused."

Marie may not have believed her own argument, but she was gratified to see that Corinna was sufficiently convinced by it to empty the glass, and then, under the maid's watchful eye, essay a few forkfuls of Carème's delicious offering. At length, satisfied, Marie removed the tray and Corinna was alone again with her thoughts and the missing necklace. But whether it was the wine, or the food, or the new reminder that Dorothée was making plans, she did not know, but she was feeling much better than before.

Darkness came to Vienna in the winter months in late afternoon. This day, the clouds heavy with snow stole what little light there was left, and deep twilight settled over the city.

Dorothée came. "I will get you out of this little cell, *chérie*. I have made complicated plans, and you must listen closely. I have brought here a traveling dress, very warm, and boots. And a bonnet.

Although it is not the most fashionable, it will do, I think."

"Dorothée, I have something I must tell you."

"Tell me then, but put your feet into the boots. I should have brought Marie—she knows how to dress one. First one foot and then the other, I should think."

"I cannot let you do this."

"*Hein?* I think you must. The entire city is buzzing with the theft of that bauble of the duchess's. I will not let that harpy get her claws into you. Let me tie the strings of this bonnet—oh, you know how that is done? *Formidable*."

Corinna was doing Dorothée's bidding, thrusting her narrow feet into the lovely soft fur-lined boots, settling the bonnet on her head, even accepting the fur-lined cloak that Dorothée had brought yesterday. But on another level in her mind she was nerving herself for her confession.

"Dorothee, listen—please listen to me. I have—" Her voice broke over a sob in her throat, and she could not speak. She picked up the reticule and opened it. "See?" she said at last. "This is the necklace! But I did not steal it—I didn't!"

"Of course you didn't. I knew that from the start, did I not tell you so?"

"Yes, you did. But I did not know I had the necklace then."

Dorothée pulled the object from the pouch and held it to the light. After a moment, she smiled faintly.

"How shall I return it to her?" Corinna asked anxiously.

"Do not try. I suppose the duchess must have arranged to insert this into your possessions in some way, which need not concern us in the least. I will put the bauble back, so. Now, *chérie*, you are ready to go. Do not talk to me of this trifling thing. Keep it—you may find a use for it if you meet a fool on your way back to London."

"London!"

"Did I not tell you I would arrange? Now, you are ready to go? Marie will have my own cloak for me, and we will start."

"I do not understand."

"Of course not. But I will tell you as we go."

With only one backward glance at the haven that, suddenly, seemed preferable to the unknown ahead, even if that road led to London, Corinna followed her friend down the stairs.

With great stealth, Dorothée and Corinna walked with a deceptive air of casualness through the unfrequented halls of the Kaunitz Palace. Corinna's blood pounded in her head. She did not know where she was going, in spite of the hurried instructions whispered in her ear as they walked.

"There will be a carriage, my own, as you can see from the panel. And there will be a stop outside the city, at a small inn. I know it well."

Most likely from some intrigue of Dorothée's that she did not wish noticed, thought Corinna, amused.

"At this inn, you will stop."

When she did not continue, Corinna asked, "Do I spend the night there? I have money."

"Of course. You have that vulgar handful of stones."

Corinna thought she detected amusement in the princess's voice.

"I think not the night. Here, let us close this door behind us. We do not wish to give notice of our departure. The carriage is on that drive over there." Corinna saw it. "I will wait here, to see you safely inside it."

There was nothing to say, Corinna thought. Or rather, there was so much to say and no words to say it in. The princess too seemed moved. She hugged Corinna quickly, and whispered, "Go now. The coachman will not like to let his horses stand."

"You are such a true friend."

"Do not hold me to ten out of ten," Dorothée said cryptically. "Perhaps four out of ten will do." She gave Corinna a little push in the direction of the carriage. "Hurry."

CHAPTER 22

The princess's carriage was excessively comfortable and extremely luxurious. Corinna sank back on the velvet squabs and thought, No fugitive from the law ever traveled in such magnificence!

She would, of course, return the necklace to the duchess, after she returned to England. She did not see her way ahead very far. In truth, she saw, and that not clearly, only the short journey outside the city to the inn her benefactor had mentioned. Of course, the carriage must go back to the princess.

Dorothée had said that other transportation would be provided. Corinna had strong doubts that she had funds sufficient for the journey, nor could she travel alone, without even an abigail. But neither could she stay in Vienna and wait for the duchess's vengeance to fall on her.

The snow had begun to fall in earnest now. She peered from the coach, hoping to catch sight of the inn. A dark shape loomed ahead, veiled by swirling snowflakes caught in the light from the carriage lamps. The pace of the horses slowed, and the coachman directed them into the innyard. At the side of the two-story building stood what appeared to be an elegant traveling coach. The other transportation? Of course.

Dorothée had not failed her yet!

A tall and bulky footman opened the coach door

and helped her out. Odd, she thought; he did not seem to be in uniform, but he was muffled to the eyebrows in greatcoat and scarf, and most likely he wore French livery underneath.

She was helped into the inn and shown into a private sitting room. Quite like an English inn, she thought. Certainly not like those she had suffered in throughout Germany!

But it made sense in a way—she must have been set on the road to Italy. That name brought up visions of orange groves and vineyards, and warm sunshine—a great contrast to the snow falling persistently, as it had since November, out of Austria's leaden skies.

She was brought a large glass of mulled wine. The warmth in her stomach was marvelously restoring, and her courage, which she had thought lost forever, returned in force. She was fortified against whatever was yet to come this night.

She could not in her wildest fancy have predicted what was to come next.

The heavy sounds of booted feet approached, and stopped outside the sitting-room door. Knuckles rapped, and at the same instant the door opened.

She stared at the newcomer. She put her hand out, the palm toward him as though to ward off a ghost. "You—"

"I had hoped," said the elegant gentleman standing before her, removing the footman's coat he had worn, "to receive a slightly warmer welcome." He looked closely at her, and in a much altered voice, said, "My dearest Corinna, I should not have startled you so. You're white as a ghost!" He shouted through the open door, "Host, bring brandy!"

"Oh, no, Justin, I shall not dare to drink anything more." She gestured toward the empty glass on the table. "In truth, I suspected you were formed out of the wine I have just finished."

"Nonetheless, you are to drink this." He took the glass from the host and held it to her lips until she was forced to drink.

Somewhat shakily, and fearfully aware of a strong buzzing in her head, she said, "How is it you are here? What of—"

"I am your other transportation. Did not her highness warn you that you would change vehicles here?"

"Yes, but Justin, she made no mention of you. I should not have come—"

"You had no choice. Your intriguing friend arranged all. My part was simply to meet you, and tell you—" All the planned rhetoric that he had worked out, all his careful explanations of his recent actions, his honorable intentions, vanished.

From his heart, he said, "Did you think you could escape me, ever?"

"No—that is, I did not think at all—but, Justin, I must tell you—what are you doing!"

"First I will shut this door, so that we may be private. And then I will take leave to remove this awkward bonnet. And then I will kiss you." He did, at length, and thoroughly.

"Justin, I cannot—"

"Ah, but you did. I have one question of you, love."

I didn't steal trembled on her lips, unspoken. The question he had in mind, however, did not refer to the necklace. "Shall we go ahead to Italy, and find some way to return to England and be married at home, or shall I take you to Lady Castlereagh, and we shall be married at once? My love, you must tell me what you wish."

She was not listening. Shaken by the vigor of his

embrace, and longing for him to continue, she pulled away. "I cannot—oh, this is all wrong!"

"My love, what is this?"

The time had come. For answer, she opened her bag and spilled out the contents on the table. Even dirty, the diamonds were impressively huge, and the rubies spread out like gouts of blood. Her vision blurred, and at first she did not recognize that her tears were flowing. Indifferently, she did not care enough even to dash them from her eyes.

"All that trouble, your fright—yes, the princess told me. And for a bauble."

"Justin! I m-mean, Lord Lonsdale—"

"What happened to *Justin*? I do like to hear my name on your lips."

She could not see him clearly through her tears, but she was aware—so very much aware—of his nearness. The clean smell of his shaving soap she recognized, the indefinable prickling as of a current, a current that spoke of living, not of a backwater—like Morland Hall.

"Bauble! There's a fortune here!"

"A fortune? My dear girl—"

"I am not your dear girl!" Her voice was muffled.

"Shortly, I will disabuse your mind of such wrongheaded ideas. But at the moment we must talk."

Talk! When all she wanted was to sob her heart out, see the end of Almira and that villain Jack Hardie, even of Emma, and simply crawl into a corner. She was so tired, and the effort of keeping Lord Lonsdale at a distance was excessively wearying.

"It is diverting, don't you think, that we might have coursed half across Europe—"

"We?"

"Of course. I should have followed you, you may

be sure of that. All on account of a few pounds of strass."

"Strass!" Strass—the man-made product often brought to such a high degrees of perfection that even kings did not cavil at wearing jewels of paste.

"Of course. Even Cousin Maria—although," he added thoughtfully, "I think I shall not claim the relationship in the future—even the duchess would not be foolish enough to fondle a king's ransom every day. I should be much surprised if her entire collection were not paste. That includes my grandmother's tiara. I told her I would not sue her for it—I am sure the one she has is a replica."

Indignation began to rise in Corinna. It was a long time since she had felt alive—but now even the prickling of anger was welcome to her.

"That woman! To think that—I cannot believe—and that little fool Almira—"

She caught herself up. If she could have taken back those last words, she would have on the instant. Almira might be a little fool, and few could be found to deny it, but she was to be the bride of the man standing now no more than a couple of feet away. So the duchess had claimed. She had more than reasonable doubts about the duchess's honesty, but this question was one that must be cleared up, now, by Justin himself.

"I could not agree with you more," said Justin. "Must we talk about Almira? I confess she bores me excessively."

"Bores you! Then how in the world do you expect to get through thirty years with her?"

His eyebrows rose. "Thirty years? I should not look with equanimity upon thirty hours with her. But my dear girl, perhaps you will tell me why you think I contemplate three decades of the most acute boredom possible?"

"You are to wed her. Surely you cannot have forgotten that fact?"

"Since," he said, irritation edging his voice, "I never knew that fact, I can scarcely have forgotten it. Where on earth did you get such a mistaken idea?"

"The duchess. She told us as soon as we arrived—"

Suddenly the expression in his eyes shook her. He was not behaving like a man betrothed to someone else. Nor, to be honest, had he ever. She had raised up a barrier between them made of paper. But it had felt like iron all the while.

There was a hunger in his face, together with a determination that caused her to consider recoiling. She stood her ground

He leaned forward, one white-knuckled hand flat on the table. "You mean the duchess told you I had offered for Almira?"

"N-not precisely offered."

"Then what?"

"I think she said—a marriage had been arranged."

The new look in his eyes kindled a glow somewhere in the region she considered her heart. He started menacingly toward her, and for a moment she waited hopefully for him to pounce on her.

"That—that blasted woman! Do you mean to tell me that you believed her? And that is why you turned me down? And that is—"

"What else could I do?" she asked innocently.

For answer he took her roughly into his arms. "You could have used the sense God gave you—"

Words failed him, and instead he rained kisses upon her upturned and receptive face. After a long and deliciously tingling time, she pulled back. Looking up, she said, "Should I not go back to Almira?"

Surprisingly, he laughed. "Almira and Cousin Maria have each other. And at another time we might find diversion in learning how they deal with each other. And with young Hardie."

"Will he marry her, do you think?"

"Dear love, no matter. They deserve each other. As for this moment, I can think of a better occupation for us!"

He drew her again to him. She felt a small thud upon her foot, and somewhere in her mind she knew that the necklace—that accursed necklace of no value—had fallen to the floor.

Absently, she kicked the bauble away, and clasped her arms more tightly around her beloved's neck.

The necklace might be paste, but what she had now was genuine, a jewel above price, and all her own.

ABOUT THE AUTHOR

Vanessa Gray grew up in Oak Park, Illinois, and graduated from the University of Chicago. She currently lives in the farm country of northeastern Indiana, where she pursues her interest in the history of Georgian England and the Middle Ages. She is the author of a number of bestselling Regencies—*The Masked Heiress, The Lonely Earl, The Wicked Guardian, The Wayward Governess, The Dutiful Daughter, The Innocent Deceiver, The Reckless Orphan* and *The Duke's Messenger*—available in Signet editions.